The Writers Block

Courtnee Howell-Turner

Pale Woods Publishing

The Writer's Block

A Contemporary Romance

Copyright © September 6, 2025

Erwin, TN

by Courtnee Howell-Turner

Library of Congress Control Number: 2025918154

Paperback IBSN 979-8-9899846-5-7

E-book IBSN 979-8-9899846-6-4

This book is a work of fiction. Names, characters, businesses, places, events, and incidents are the product of the author's imagination or used in a fictitious manner. Any similarities or resemblance to actual persons, living or dead, events, or places is entirely coincidental.

Cover Design: Taylor Dawn, Sweet15 Designs, LLC

Other Titles by Courtnee

PARANORMAL MYSTERY

My Brother's Keeper

Pinky Swear

Rose Colored Glasses

Appalachian Mystery

The Secret Lives of Copperheads and Fireflies

ROMANCE

FINDING EMMA

FINDING DAVID

FINDING MRS. WINSOME

PARANORMAL SUSPENSE

Solomon's Tears

THRILLER

Hollis's Hobby

The Tears on the Water

FANTASY

Cascade

Under Archard's Dome

MIDDLE-GRADE MYSTERY AND SUSPENSE

Rasputin's Scorn

COLORING BOOK

Pale Woods Haunted Houses

JOURNAL

Anxiety/Religious Journal

The Writers Block Playlist

"Chapstick" COIN

"Saturday" Twenty-One Pilots

"Counting Stars" One Republic

"Fireflies" Owl City

"Sky Full of Stars" Coldplay

"When You Were Young" The Killers

"Champange Supernova" Oasis

"The Kill" Thirty Seconds to Mars

"Viva la Vida" Coldplay

"Manchild" Sabrina Carpenter

"Adventure of a Lifetime" Coldplay

"Payphone" Maroon 5

"Paradise" Coldplay

"Clocks" Coldplay

"Vanilla Twilight" Owl City

"Yellow" Coldplay

A Note to Readers

Dear People Who Enjoy the Written Word,

When my mama was pregnant with me, she wanted to name me Melody Page Turner. When I was older, the irony of the middle and last names hit me.

I have always loved to read, and now I also enjoy writing. My mama must have known something, or she was knee-deep in her own pile of books.

She named me Courtnee, but I've always wondered what it would have been like to have been called Melody Page. I guess I'll never know.

This book was ready for readers for years before I was ready to publish it. Now that I have legally adopted a new last name, I thought it was a good time to release the story.

You'll meet at least one character from another one of my novels. I hope you can spot him.

Going forward, you can find my books under Courtnee Howell-Turner. My two last names honor two men in my life, my daddy and pap-paw, who didn't have to love me – but they did.

I hope you enjoy the book. If so, please leave a review. Also, reach out to me and let me know your favorite part.

Your friend in the written world,
Courtnee

Content Warning

This story touches on post-traumatic stress disorder (PTSD) that resulted from a past abusive relationship. It includes flashbacks and anxiety. While the story does not focus on her past, Paige's experiences have shaped her as a character.

I also write about two episodes of domestic abuse. Readers who are sensitive to similar situations may want to read one of my other selections.

If you are a victim of domestic violence, I hope you know you have options. Please call this number if you need help leaving you current circumstances: 1-800-799-7233.

Chapter 1

Paige sat in front of her laptop, chewing an unsharpened pencil.

"I'll send Gilbert to Morocco, and I'll bring back Robert," she said to herself.

Her voice echoed off the walls of her tiny cottage. It was barely five rooms of livable space, but she only needed the corner of the living room to immerse herself in her work. She hardly slept in her bedroom, preferring instead to crash on the couch. It was closer to her writing space.

She'd had a difficult time writing, and even though she loved her craft, it was hard to determine a direction. In six books, her characters had been through almost every trying situation possible, and she was afraid her seventh book would have to wrap up their tangled affair. Her characters were her comfort, though, and she wasn't ready to leave Autumn, April, Gilbert, and Robert to start a new series with characters she'd have to form over time.

Before she'd finished her last book, she wrote every day, sometimes writing more than five thousand words a day. Of course, that was slaughtered by the editor, but she still woke up every day with a strong purpose to move her characters through their lives.

Over the past month, it had been different. She saw the trajectory of the romances she'd created, and she knew it was time to give her readers a happy ending, even if wasn't the one they wanted. It was hard to lead the people she had created to the end of their stories, and she wasn't ready to part with them.

Paige gulped down the rest of her water. She drank everything quickly. At parties, she was the first one to get wild and pass out. She always had the most interesting times she couldn't remember, but her friends were happy to fill her in on the details later.

I need a break, she thought to herself.

She picked up her keys and headed out her door. She had a passing thought to lock it, but she lived in a town with a low crime rate, and her destination was only a block away.

She walked into a beautiful autumn day. The sky held a cornflower blue shade, and no clouds were in sight. Her elongated shadow reminded her of the upcoming time change, and she inwardly sighed.

Paige didn't like the darker evenings. Once the sun had set, it took her productivity with it. Unlike most writers, Paige was more constructive in the spring and summer months, while the sun reigned throughout most of her waking hours.

The afternoon light felt muted, and even though it was only two o'clock, it seemed much later. The sun was moving away from her spot in the world, and she'd miss its heightened warmth.

Her phone dinged. She glanced at the screen and saw a notification about a writer in her publishing group.

"Greg made a post," she mumbled.

A couple passing her on the sidewalk stared at her strangely and hurried past. Most people in the town were used to her peculiar ways, but she'd never seen the people, so they were probably from out of town.

She debated looking at it right away, but she decided to save it until she could give it her full attention. Greg hardly ever posted anything on social media, so she wanted to support him. It wasn't a requirement within her small but elite publishing circle, but the authors usually did it.

Paige smelled the coffee shop before she walked through its open door. The same wood lined the floors and walls. She didn't know the name, but the heels on her boots made satisfying clicks against the planks' polished surface.

A mom and her son leaned against the counter as she decided on her beverage. The little boy danced around, littering crumbs on the floor at their feet.

Laura waved her over. "Hey, Paige! What can I get you?"

Paige didn't like coffee. The only reason she came into the coffee shop was to see Laura.

"I'll have a mango smoothie."

She stayed several feet away from the woman and her son. The woman seemed to notice and scolded her child for breaking his bread across the floor. She ordered a plain coffee, and they left before Laura handed Paige her smoothie.

"Where's your broom?" Paige asked her.

Laura looked at the floor, spotting the mess. "Oh, I'll get it."

She brought out a broom and dustpan, tending to the mess the careless child had left behind. She finished quickly and returned to her spot behind the glass display, where doughnuts and large cinnamon rolls tempted Paige's bank account and waistline.

Paige took a sip of her smoothie. "Doesn't that bother you?"

Laura's eyebrows went up. "The mess?" She shook her head. "No. The little boy had a cold last week, and he couldn't have a muffin, but he felt better today, so I gave him one. Did you hear him humming as he ate it?"

Laura's eyes lit up as she told Paige the story, but Paige only smiled and nodded.

"I think it was a little rude of his mother to leave you with the mess."

Paige picked up a newspaper and glass cleaner and wiped fingerprints from the glass case. She had shared with Paige that newspapers worked better than paper towels for leaving a streak-free shine.

"I don't mind." She swatted Paige playfully with the newspaper. "I like children, unlike some people."

"I like children," Paige defended. "I'm just not a fan of their whininess or messes."

"That'll all change when you have one," Laura returned.

Paige strongly disagreed, but she kept her feelings to herself. Laura and her husband had been trying to have children for several years, but Laura's work schedule at her new business and the stress from his job had kept them childless.

Paige wished her friend could get pregnant. She'd never met a more perfect couple than Laura and Rob, and if anyone deserved to have children, it was them.

"Aren't you supposed to be writing?" Laura asked.

Paige took another sip of her smoothie. She was pretty certain Laura had added an extra mango, and it tasted divine.

"I can't decide whether I want to bring Robert back."

Laura grabbed her hand. "Oh, please do it!"

Paige shook her head at her friend's enthusiasm. They'd met at a book signing years ago, as Laura had read all of Paige's books. After a long conversation, Paige invited her to become a beta reader, and their relationship had grown.

"I like people to stay dead when I kill them."

Laura laughed. "Sure. But they never found his body."

"The plane was utterly destroyed," she countered.

Laura raised her eyebrows and adopted an eerie tone. "But they never found the body."

A group of patrons walked through the door, and Paige tried to pay Laura for the smoothie before they reached the counter. Laura batted her money away.

Paige pushed the money back to her. "You support my business, so I can support yours."

Laura whispered to her. "I read your books for free, so the smoothies are complimentary."

Paige gave up, stuffing the money into her pocket. "Okay, but I'm going to quit coming here if you won't let me pay you."

Laura batted her eyes. "I'm always here, and you couldn't stand to be away from me for that long."

Paige conceded the point and made her way back out into the afternoon air. A crisp breeze blew between the main street buildings, and she pulled her light coat tightly against her.

Once she'd walked back to her small house, she checked the mailbox. It had been empty for almost a week. Either her mailman had forgotten her, or Paige had gotten so reclusive that the rest of the world didn't think she existed. A quick look at her phone calmed the latter fear, as she had accumulated nine text messages and three emails since she'd taken a break. Most of the messages had an easy answer, and her fingers moved quickly across the keys. The last one she addressed was from her publisher.

Daisey asked her to call or come by the office. Since Daisey's office was an hour away, Paige opted to call her.

She picked up after the first ring. "Daisey Flower Publications."

Paige rolled her eyes at the formal greeting. "It's me, Daisey. It should have shown up on your caller ID."

There was a pause. "It probably did, but I'm a little busy. Let me get straight to the point."

At the business's foundation, Daisy had bought the small company from a local woman with a few clients. She ran it as a hybrid press, asking writers to pay for the first five hundred books she printed to recoup her editing, design, and formatting costs. At first, her business was small, but after someone murdered her husband, Daisey's social media following grew, and people bought more of the books she promoted.

Daisey saw a trend in mystery, romance, and crime novels, so she collected the most promising writers in the southeastern region of the United States to help her make a bigger name for herself in the publishing industry. It worked. Before long, people were raving about her books, and she made enough money to offer authors paid contracts.

Then Daisey had an affair with one of her writers, and Daisy Flower Publications became a household name. When she gave birth to the man's child, they stayed together for a while. They split up, resulting in a terrible custody battle, and like she always did, Daisey got her way. The child was five, and to Paige's knowledge, Daisey had only allowed her to see her father for a handful of holidays and weekends in the last two years. The ongoing drama between the writer and Daisey added spice to the company's name, and millions knew about it.

"Okay, doll. So, I need a favor."

Paige had learned that her boss's "favors" were usually pretty big. She braced herself.

"I need you to do an interview."

Paige was more than happy to supply her publisher with pages upon pages of an almost perfectly polished manuscript, but she balked at public appearances. So far, other than one terribly failed television interview, Paige had gotten by with pre-recorded interviews she posted on social media. She had a considerable following, so her face and plans for future novels seemed to reach the right audience.

She opened her mouth to protest, but Daisey spoke over her. "Listen, doll. I know you fell on your face once, but you've got to pull yourself up and move on."

Daisey hardly ever doled out terms of endearment, so the interview was a big deal to her. Still, Paige was apprehensive about appearing live.

"I thought we discussed this. I can't do live TV."

"Sweetheart, it's not just about you. I've put together a few of my headliners, so you'll just be a face in the crowd."

Paige relaxed a little. "The focus won't be just on me?"

"No, doll. You'll have a little time to tell about your work, but everyone else will be busy talking, so you'll be another pretty face."

"I don't know that I like—"

"Oh, I'm sorry, doll. I forgot you were a feminist." She took a drink of something and swallowed audibly. "You'll be there to support your fellow authors and Daisey Flowers Publications."

"I guess—"

"Then it's settled," Daisey said swiftly. "The interview will be next Thursday morning. Be certain to be at the news studio in Johnson City by five o'clock."

"Five o'clock!" Paige said. "I don't usually go to sleep until two—"

"Yes, of course, doll," her publisher interrupted. "You'll just have to turn in early that night. You don't want to have puffies around your eyes on live television."

Paige was stunned into silence, automatically telling her employer goodbye before she was ready. As they ended the call, Paige thought of something to ask.

"Who else will be there?"

Daisey was gone, ending the call quickly, as she did every time. Paige took her phone away from her ear and stared at it.

Paige was going to do a live interview. She only hoped it wasn't as disastrous as her last one.

Chapter 2

Paige lay against her pillow, reclining on the couch, and scrolling through her social media feed. She commented on a handful of posts by authors she recognized in hopes they'd return the favor.

She thought about her earlier notification and looked up Greg's profile. He didn't post a lot, electing to put news about his book signings as his only public footprint. He'd added a picture of a plane ticket to the Blountville airport with a song by Rusted Root. The caption read: *I'm on my way to the Tri-Cities!*

"He should have been more specific," she mumbled. "There's more than just one Tri-City area, and it would have been cheaper to fly into Knoxville or Asheville."

She liked the post and entered her comment. *It will be so good to see you again!*

She tried not to count the minutes until her phone notified her of a response. Greg had typed: *I can't wait!*

Paige scrutinized his reply. *Did he mean he couldn't wait to see her, or was he just excited about visiting the area again?*

She turned off the light, hoping her mind would shut down. She turned her pillow over three times, but thoughts about Greg still plagued her.

They had followed each other on social media for over a year, exchanging professional congratulatory remarks and passing humorous banter over funny memes. She had messaged him after the last hurricane that had struck his area, and he had asked about her health after surgery.

She turned her phone back on and stared at his profile picture. *He just values you as a professional,* she told herself.

That didn't stop her from staring at his raven-black hair, brown eyes, and perfectly maintained beard. In the picture, his toned arms rested casually on the table before him, and even though he slouched a little, he was clearly over six feet tall.

"Tall, dark, and handsome," she said to her empty living room.

She turned off her phone.

She'd be professional when she met him. She'd shake his hand and congratulate him on his newest book release.

She wouldn't let Greg Salem know she had one of the most serious crushes on him she'd ever had in her life.

***

"You'll be fine," Laura assured her. "The interview will only last a few minutes, and you'll get to meet Mary Ruby."

Laura was easily star-struck. Paige thought the news anchor was pretty but seemed to favor wealthy businessmen. That alone didn't bother Paige, but Mary Ruby had broken up a few marriages before deciding she didn't want to be with the men whose homes she ruined.

"Yeah," Paige remarked in a deadpan. "That'll be a hoot."

Laura hit her with the hand towel she'd been using to wipe down the counter. "Don't be so hard on her. I hear that she's a nice lady."

Paige stirred her smoothie with a straw. "Your strawberry smoothies may be the best ones on your menu."

Laura waited to answer until a customer had swiped his card. Paige watched over him to make sure he left Laura a tip.

"Rob came up with the recipe. I add a little more—"

Paige held up her hand. "Don't tell me. If you do, I'll taste the individual ingredients instead of getting the full effect."

Laura leaned over the counter, whispering conspiratorially to Paige. "Do you think he'll be there?"

Paige didn't have to ask who she meant. It seemed the entire world knew his name.

"Evan Donaldson is everywhere he needs to be." She laughed at her use of the famous writer's catchphrase.

Laura waggled her eyebrows. "Do you think he'll see Daisey while he's here?"

Paige shook her head. "Not if he can help it. He'll try to arrange to see Petal, but who knows if Daisey will let him."

Laura stood up straight as another customer asked for an order. She handed him a bag of doughnuts, and the sweet glaze wafted through the air, almost overpowering the rich coffee scent that lingered.

"My wife loves these," he told Laura. "She's pregnant, and they've been her only craving."

Paige noticed Laura look away before she turned on an extra bright smile. "I'm so glad she and the baby enjoy them."

After the customer left, Paige sat silently while Laura pretended that sorting her perfectly lined baked goods was of the utmost importance. Finally, Paige knew she'd have to say something, or she'd burst.

"Have you visited an infertility doctor yet?"

Laura winced and checked to make sure her seated customers weren't within earshot. "We went, but they can't find anything wrong with us. The doctor offered to prescribe shots of a hormone to help boost our chances of getting pregnant, but my emotions are already haywire, so I told him we'd wait."

There was an uncomfortable silence where Paige debated the proper response. "I hope you get what you want."

Laura's mood changed, and Paige sensed a mischievous comment. "I hope you get what you want, too."

Paige almost choked on her smoothie. "What's that supposed to mean?"

"Greg Salem."

It was Paige's turn to look around the room. Everyone was chattering, oblivious to her embarrassment.

"I should never have told you."

Laura crossed her arms, a triumphant grin spreading across her face. "Then you shouldn't have had so much to drink at my last party."

It was true. Paige had been going through a miserable breakup, and Greg's post had shown up on her feed as she was wallowing in self-pity.

"Isn't he a beautiful man?" she'd asked Laura. "Why couldn't I end up with someone who is handsome and smart?"

Rob had heard her, and he had leaned his head into the room. "Because I'm already taken." He smiled widely, waiting for his joke to be acknowledged.

Laura shooed away her husband and placed a hand on Paige's arm. "You will. It may or may not be him" — she nodded to Greg's face on Paige's screen — "but you'll find someone perfect for you."

Paige's attention returned to her surroundings. Chairs scraped against the floor, signaling the end of the breakfast crowd. Laura had half an hour to prepare before businesses dismissed their employees for lunch, and she needed every moment of the time to make the necessary adjustments.

Paige stuffed a twenty-dollar bill into her friend's tip jar when she wasn't looking. Laura handed her a bag of the doughnuts she'd smelled.

Paige held up the bag. "I can't eat these. The camera adds ten pounds—"

Laura interrupted her. "Good. You need it."

She didn't argue with her friend. She took the doughnuts to her house, and after she'd stared at her cursor blinking for half an hour, she ate all of them.

Chapter 3

Paige's heels clicked against the tile as she crossed the lobby. The receptionist directed her to a long hallway, telling her that the waiting room was at the end.

He was already there when she opened the door.

Her heart leaped into her throat before she could swallow it back down. He stood up and cocked his head to the side.

"Are you going to shut the door?"

She glanced at the knob and let go of it quickly. The heavy wood banged closed behind her.

Finally, she was alone with him. She searched for something to say, but the professional platitudes flew out of her mind before she could grab them.

Greg crossed the distance between them, and as she stuck out her hand, he brought her in for a hug. "You look beautiful."

Paige opened her mouth, and some words fell out. "You smell nice."

She tensed as soon as she'd said it. *What had she been thinking?* She should have just accepted his compliment and moved on to the next topic of conversation.

He pulled out of the embrace enough to stare at her. His chocolate eyes melted any chance she had to recover gracefully. She could feel his arms flex around her, strong and sure.

Greg chuckled good-naturedly. "I think it's just the hotel soap. I was in a rush, and I forgot my cologne."

The hug ended just as she was getting used to it. Then, the uncomfortable moment arrived when she'd have to choose a seat.

The room was small, with a table of fruit and muffins on one end, and several couches and chairs lining the remaining walls. Greg had been sitting on the sofa with a clear view of the door, and there wasn't a seat available that would keep her within comfortable talking distance of him. She didn't want to seem like she was alienating him, but she was careful not to be presumptuous by selecting a seat beside him.

She took her place on the couch first. To her surprise, he chose a chair opposite her. They could still speak, but their conversation would be much louder. It was the way friends and colleagues spoke and lacked the intimacy she desired.

He had dressed in black pants and a white button-up shirt. He had undone the top button, and her mind wandered to what it would be like to pull the shirt off him.

He was staring at her, and it brought her back. "What?"

"I said, congratulations on The New Way," he repeated.

The New Way was her most recent release, even though she'd written it a year ago. She accepted his accolades and tried to remember the name of the last book he'd released.

In a moment of panic, her mind went blank. She tried to recall the title, but it was like trying to grab fog.

Come on, she begged her stymied brain. *Remember the name. You wrote the blurb for the back cover, for goodness' sake!*

She had enough time to notice a look pass across Greg's face that seemed a lot like hurt before the door opened. A man with a dark suit, bottle-blond hair, and startling blue eyes joined them.

"Evan!" Greg greeted him, embracing him as he had Paige.

Her heart sank when she saw the same familiarity in their exchange. She straightened her spine and reminded herself to be more professional.

Evan sat beside her, and a sheet of paper wouldn't have fit between them. Paige tried to edge away without making her moves noticeable, but Evan grabbed her around the waist and pecked her lips.

"You look amazing, Paige, my dear. I was so happy to hear you got away from that sad what's-his-face."

Paige regained her composure when he released her. So much for professionalism with Evan around. He crossed every boundary, like he was cutting through tape with a chainsaw.

The door opened again, and Mary Ruby entered the room. Her platinum hair and bright smile transfixed everyone. Her long, tan legs and trim physique didn't make her hard to look at either.

Evan bounced off the couch and took Mary's hand. "How is the jewel of Johnson City this morning?"

She had competed in beauty pageants, but once she became one of the leading news anchors in the region, she turned in her tiara for local fame and scores of men. She seemed to be happy, as there were people in the area who prided themselves on their ability to sniff out depression or a drug problem, and Mary had neither.

Her only response was to allow Evan's touch, and without seeing anything more, Paige knew they'd slept together. Mary's eyes hardly left him as she ran through the general interview procedure.

Evan touched the small of her back as she led the group to the room where the interview would take place. On television, the room had seemed bigger, and Paige could almost envision a studio audience looking on as Mary conducted interviews, but seeing the room from the other side of the lens took all the glamor away. It almost made the area seem sterile.

"Is it just us?" Paige asked.

Mary turned her profile, but her body kept moving to her seat. "Daisey will be here when we start."

Paige understood the reason. If her publisher had to be in the same room with Evan for longer than ten minutes, her professional demeanor crumbled. Evan could make Daisey lose her cool, and to Paige's knowledge, no one else could do it.

They moved to a matching couch and a chair beside Mary's desk. Paige took the chair, but Mary directed her to the couch.

"It will look better on camera if you're sandwiched between the boys," she said. Assuming that Daisey would take the chair, she put Greg in the seat next to the chair.

Paige fully understood that the arrangement was to benefit Daisey, and she was thankful for it. The new seating arrangement allowed her to sit close to Greg.

Mary signaled to one of the cameramen, and he returned with Daisey. She took her seat gracefully, staring straight at Mary.

She'd dressed in a navy-blue business suit, accentuating her ample breasts. Her premature silver hair shone under the stage lights, giving her blue eyes an undeniable sparkle. She exuded confidence, and her posture suggested she was completely at ease in front of the camera.

Evan waved at his ex-girlfriend, but she ignored him. He laughed and sat back on the couch.

A man counted numbers back, and they were live. Paige hadn't had the opportunity to assess her stage fright until that moment, and suddenly everything came into sharper focus.

Mary was talking, going over the merits of the company and each author, but all Paige could think about were the hundreds of people watching them. What were they seeing when they looked at her on-screen? She certainly didn't appear confident or sexy like the two other women in the room. She was average at best, with auburn hair, light skin, and a rash of freckles.

As Paige tried to rub her sweaty hands on the couch's fabric casually, Mary asked Daisey why she chose to interview with the local station. "A bigger news outlet would have given you a broader reach."

It seemed Daisey already had an answer prepared. "Yes, Mary, but we owe our success to the people in the community who were our first readers and followers. They deserve to hear our big news first."

What big news? Paige thought. Daisy hadn't mentioned anything specific when she'd spoken to her. Evan and Greg seemed equally baffled, so Paige didn't feel so alone.

"Speaking of local, you brought an author from this area with you today."

Daisey took Mary's cue. "Yes, I did. Paige Turner is from Erwin, and she writes romances that center in her hometown."

"Paige Turner?" Mary questioned as if she'd never heard Paige's full name. "Is that a pseudonym?"

It was a common question, but as she'd explained in her prerecorded interviews and over social media, it was her real name.

"No, it's my name," she replied. "My mother had a weird sense of humor."

In truth, her mother probably hadn't thought about the hilarity of the combination until Paige was in school. She lived up to the irony of her name by reading stacks of books and becoming a writer.

"Well, that's fortuitous," Mary replied. "Can you tell us a little about your series?"

It was Paige's moment to promote her work, but her tongue felt heavy. *Why would anyone want to hear about the romantic triangle between April, Robert, and Gilbert?*

Her hesitation was just long enough to make Mary raise her eyebrows and laugh nervously.

Evan rushed in to save her. "The poor darling suffers from impersonation syndrome. She's highly successful, but she has a hard time believing she deserves it."

Paige's pride swelled. Evan was an amazing author with a USA Today author tag, and he had complimented her.

"It's *imposter* syndrome," Daisey corrected. Her words were cool, and her extra-wide smile stretched. "But she has a lovely series of romance novels, one of which we've made into an audiobook and screenplay."

Daisey was toying with new ideas to further her business, and she believed making in-house audiobooks were another good option for her readers. She planned to make all of her offerings available in that format, but the proper equipment and voice talent were expensive, and the process was tedious and time-consuming.

The attention was around her instead of on her, and Paige took a deep breath. Greg's fingers tickled the palm of her hand, and when she stole a glance at him, he gave her an encouraging smile.

Paige found her voice and spoke about her series. She tried to imagine them all gathered around her kitchen table, talking and drinking wine, instead of speaking in front of hundreds of viewers.

"Would you say your work is character-driven?" Mary asked.

"Very much so," Paige answered. "My characters speak to me, and I am only a conduit through which they talk to the world."

She wanted to cringe after she'd said it, and a bit of her stage fright returned. Thankfully, her portion of the interview was over, and Mary moved on to Greg.

"Greg, you write mysteries, don't you?"

His hand moved away from her and fell into his lap. "Yes, Mary. I have authored two different mystery—"

Mary interrupted him by holding up a book lying on her desk. Paige couldn't remember if Mary had shown one of her books while she was speaking.

Greg nodded at the book like he was greeting an old friend. "That was my first novel."

"I've read it," Mary admitted, smiling sheepishly. "I slept with the lights on for a week."

"It was based on some true events in my home state, so you may have had a good reason to feel that way."

She returned the book to its place on her desk. "Speaking of home states, you live in Florida. How did you develop a business partnership with Daisey Flowers Publications?"

"I contacted Daisey when I had the premise for my second novel." He laughed nervously. "I probably shouldn't admit this since I'm from Florida, but I'm a UT football fan."

Mary smiled benignly. "I doubt any of our viewers will fault you for that."

His eyes crinkled at the corners. "You're probably right, but if I want to go back home without getting booed as I walk down the street, I have to keep it a secret."

"Your secret is safe with me," Mary said, miming zipping her mouth closed.

"Well," he went on, "I had written a story about a murder on the football team, and I thought it would interest Daisey."

Daisey jumped in without missing a beat. "I loved it. Greg knows how to do his research, and his endings always have a surprise twist."

For some reason, that hit Paige's ego. She was known for surprise endings. Inwardly, she reflected it was fine for her and Greg to be known for the same thing. But Mary and Daisey hadn't mentioned it during her part of the interview.

"I'm known for twists," Evan piped up. "In the sheets."

"We all know that," Mary said, holding up his latest book.

A woman and two men held each other in a carnal embrace as they stared out from behind a stream of water. The cover was tantalizing enough, but the story was purely erotic.

"You write reverse harem novels," Mary said.

Evan nodded along as she spoke. "As you well know."

Unwilling to admit their fraternization on public television, Mary's smile faltered. She addressed Daisey next.

"What attracted you to Evan?"

Her slip was almost literal. Her mouth moved without sound until she found a way to recover.

"What did you like about Evan's writing?"

As Daisey opened her mouth to speak, Evan took over. It surprised Paige that it had taken him that long.

"She loved it for the same reason my other readers enjoy it." His eyebrows moved up and down.

Mary returned her attention to him. "Do you ever run out of material?" Color blossomed on her cheeks. "I mean, I've not read any of your books that have similar" — she paused, looking for the right word — "scenes."

"There's a reason I don't have any trouble with that," he responded, leaning up like he had a secret to share. "I have too much experience to run out of material." He winked at Mary.

Paige willed herself not to roll her eyes. It was a Herculean effort.

Evan was only a little older than her, and although he wished to exude European confidence, he was no James Bond. Paige suspected he had his own insecurities that he covered with his monster ego.

"Florida," Mary spoke suddenly, breaking the connection between Evan and her. "You're from Florida, too."

"Aye," he answered. "I was born in Johnson City, but I moved to Orlando after—"

He drew out the silence, and Paige recognized his attempt to make a jab at Daisey. Evan shook his head and adopted another approach.

"Anyway, you know how Florida boys love Tennessee girls, so Greg and I jumped at the chance to come up and have some fun."

This time, Paige rolled her eyes at his overconfidence, but she did it away from the camera. Evan had just assumed that he could go anywhere in the area and that the women who had watched the show would be lining up to leave with him.

She looked at Greg to see if he'd reacted to Evan's statement. He stared at him politely but showed no sign of agreement. She doubted Greg would be Evan's wingman, even though Evan had implied it.

Mary directed her attention to Daisey. "When you called me about the interview, you said that you had some news to share with our viewers."

Daisey launched into a spiel. She was a true businesswoman, and she spoke of her continued success and a few new releases by other authors in their group. Finally, with a side eye at the authors with her, Daisey revealed her vision.

"The three authors I have with me are some of the best in their genres. I have an idea for a new book, and they have agreed to write it."

Paige couldn't land on the part of her declaration that bothered her the most. Even Evan seemed stunned into silence. Paige couldn't remember agreeing to do anything, and by the look on the faces of the men who flanked her, they were completely blindsided.

Mary clapped her hands together. "That's going to be fantastic! When do you expect it will be released?"

Daisey was careful not to look at the authors who were staring daggers at her. "I expect it will be finished by the start of summer, and I know these writers have fans who are going to be dying to read the book, so I'm going to push the production to have it out by next September."

Just in time for the Christmas buying season, Paige thought.

The interview continued around her. After Paige had frozen, Mary was hesitant to ask her any more direct questions.

"Are you excited about this new project?" Mary asked Greg.

Her question startled him, as he was probably processing the ramifications of the proposal. "I sure am." He turned on a forced smile. "I can't wait to get started."

"I guess that will mean a lot of trips back to the Tri-Cities," Mary said, beaming at Evan.

"They can work remotely," Daisey chimed in. "Daisey Flowers Publications pays for several services, and they can choose any of them to brainstorm their contributions to the plot."

Mary was crestfallen by her answer, but she maintained her professionalism. "What is the plot?"

Daisey held up her hands. "You'd have to ask them. They've been secretive about it. But we've got a mystery writer and two romance authors coming together for a novel, so it should be exceptional."

Secretive? Up until three minutes ago, the three of them hadn't had a clue about Daisey's big news.

By the time the interview was over, Paige was almost numb. She lifted out of her seat and watched the people in front of her move until they were back in the waiting room. Daisey didn't accompany them. She left quickly, even though Evan called after her, mentioning his scheduled time with Petal.

Mary left them there, as they were expected to collect their things and leave, but none of them moved until Evan started pacing. Tensions had been building since Daisey's announcement, and Evan was the first to erupt.

"The nerve of that woman!" He ran a hand through his hair, dislodging the pile of blond curls. "She knew we couldn't refuse if it was aired on public television!"

Greg put his hand on Evan's shoulder. "But she did it on a local news show. We can still back out."

"How?" Greg asked, resuming his trip from the table to the seating area. "One of our biggest fan bases is in Northeast Tennessee and Southwest Virginia."

"They won't stay disappointed," Greg insisted. "We'll each keep putting out good books, and they have to—"

Evan wasn't listening. "I was supposed to go to Cabo in January. Do you know how long I've been planning that trip?"

"You're not hearing me, man," Greg said, attempting to get his attention by walking with him. "We don't have to write the book."

Suddenly, Paige wanted to write the book. She couldn't think of anything better than forced interaction with Greg.

"I think we should write it."

Both men stopped and looked at her. She was surprised that her small voice had caused them to pause.

"Do you think we could write it in nine months?" Greg asked.

"I know *I* can," Paige answered. Secretly, she was unsure, but Greg and Evan didn't need to know about her mild case of writer's block.

"Oh, that's just great," Evan voiced. "The two of you are all chummy about the prospect of writing together, so if I don't do it, I'll look like a jerk."

Paige raised her eyebrows. "So, are we ready to write a book together?"

"I'm in," Greg responded immediately.

Evan rolled his eyes. "I guess I'll do it, but this book is going to have so much spice it will burn your tongues."

"That's fine," Greg agreed.

"What about you, Miss Clean Romance?" Evan demanded. "Are you ready for some heat between the sheets?"

Paige shrugged. After all, it would be clear to her readers who had written the steamier parts of the novel.

"Okay, then, I guess we're writing together," Even said.

"You don't have to do it," Greg told him. "Paige and I can put it together."

Even shook his head and fixed his hair in the small mirror. "No, I'll write with you. If I didn't, you two would write a book that topped the charts." He turned around and gave a wink. "And I can't have that."

Greg looked at her, his cheeks full of more lively color than Paige had ever seen on him. "I guess we're writing a book together."

Even though his statement could have been directed at both her and Evan, Paige stared into his enigmatic eyes and felt like he was only speaking to her.

Chapter 4

"I can't believe you're writing a book with Evan Donaldson," Laura squealed.

A few of the noonday customers looked up. Once they assessed that there was no trouble, they returned to their meals and coffees.

"Not yet," Paige said, sampling her blueberry smoothie. "We haven't even agreed on a plot."

"I've read all of his books," she gushed, her brown ponytail coming loose as she talked.

"So has every other woman in America," Paige grumbled.

Laura forced a pout. "That's not like you. Usually, you support your fellow authors, especially the ones in your group."

Paige let out a sigh that didn't release any of the tension she'd felt since Daisey had announced the new project publicly. "I should be nicer, but he's an—"

"Can I have a few blueberry muffins?" a customer interrupted, pointing to the baked goods in the case.

"How many is a few?" Laura asked sweetly.

He took some time to decide, and in those seconds, Paige measured his strong build, dark hair, and blue eyes. The man was clean-shaven, and his skin was blemish-free. Catching her eye, he winked casually.

Paige blushed, hiding some of her embarrassment by drinking her smoothie. She'd not gotten caught staring at a stranger before that moment, and she spent countless hours at the mall or in the street, examining people's mannerisms.

Once he saw he had her attention, the man did his mental math aloud. "I need one for my mom, and one for each of her nurses, so I'll take four." He smiled and whispered to Paige, "I've gotta have one, too."

Paige's face was on fire, but she managed to nod. She felt like her breaths were as loud as whistles, and she hoped her stomach wouldn't grumble.

Laura put the blueberry muffins in a bag and told him the price. "I'm sorry your mom is sick."

"She's not sick," he returned.

Laura backpedaled. "You said you needed muffins for her nurses, so I—"

"She's at an assisted living facility," he told her. "I like to bring her something every time I visit."

Laura handed him a receipt, and he asked her for a pen. After he jotted something on the back, he handed the receipt to Paige.

"You can close your mouth now," Laura said when he was gone. She picked the paper from Paige's fingertips. "His name is Bobby."

Paige shrugged. "He was cute, but—"

Laura grabbed Paige's phone from the counter. She danced away from Paige when she tried to get it back.

Paige settled back onto the barstool. "It's password protected. You won't be able to get into it."

Laura measured her, holding the phone in one hand and Bobby's phone number in the other. "It's your birthday, right? The passcode is your birthday."

Paige tried to assume a blank expression, but it miffed her that her code had been so easy to guess. She sat calmly. Even though her friend had easily gotten past her code, Paige still held a trump card.

"You don't sound like me," she said triumphantly. She thought that would end her friend's meddling, but Laura typed furiously.

"It won't matter if he doesn't hear a voice." She batted her eyes at Paige.

Paige jumped for her phone, but not before Laura sent the message. Laura backed away a step, easily dodging Paige's hand.

The phone buzzed, and the women stared at it. Laura handed it to Paige.

Paige didn't try to control her annoyance. "You're not going to read it, too?"

Laura shrugged, completely unaffected. "It's your phone."

Paige didn't want to look at the message, but Laura expected to hear Bobby's response. She read Laura's message first and cringed at the lack of punctuation. At least she'd spelled everything correctly.

Laura had written that it had been nice to meet him and asked him out on a coffee date. Paige raised her eyebrows.

"I don't drink coffee."

Laura grinned sheepishly. "Yeah, but I can fix you something else when you get here."

"Who says we'd come here?" Paige returned, throwing her nose in the air. "The owner is too concerned about the lives of her patrons to remember the goods in the oven."

Laura's eyes grew wide. "The Sock-It-To-Me Cake!"

She ran into the back and returned with a self-satisfied smile. "I saved it." Going back to their previous discussion, she added, "And you guys will come here for coffee because this is the best coffee shop in town."

Laura had pulled her hair up more tightly when she ran back to the kitchen, but it fell as she swung her head. Hair bands were no match for her thick curls.

"Not if he invites me to dinner."

Laura put her hands on her hips. "You already read it?"

Paige flashed her phone screen. "Yeah. I looked over it when you were saving your cake. All he said was I should be treated to more than a cup of coffee. He told me he's a chef, and he invited me to his house for dinner."

Laura's eyebrows went up. "Don't you think you should go somewhere a little more public on a first date? What if he's a serial killer?"

Paige laughed. "A serial killer came in here to get his mother some muffins. I don't think so. Besides, how many serial killers live in Erwin?"

Laura was unconvinced. "There was that weird case that involved a teacher," she said with a smile. "And murderers can love their mamas."

Paige stared at the screen. "I guess you're right. I don't think he's a killer, but I don't want to send the wrong message either. If I go to his house, he might think he's getting lucky."

"No chance of that," Laura commented.

"What do you mean?"

Laura leaned in, whispering her answer. "You're a bit of a prude."

Paige almost spit her smoothie onto the counter. "I am not. I just got out of a three-year relationship."

"And I'm sure you had sex," Laura said, "but I never heard about it."

Paige's eyebrows drew together. "It's not exactly a conversation starter."

"Why not?" Laura asked. "We've been friends for years, and I don't know your favorite position."

Heat exploded from her chest, traveling up her neck. "I-I—"

Laura pointed at her. "My point exactly. I bet you know mine, though."

Laura had been very vocal about the positions she and Rob enjoyed, but Paige had tried not to participate in those conversations. She'd usually steer their talk away to something more agreeable.

Laura sighed heavily. "You're a romance writer, for goodness sake!"

"I write *sweet* romance."

"Uh!" Laura threw her hands up. "Don't you see what I'm trying to say?"

Paige stared at her hands. "Yeah. I know I don't like to talk about sex, but that shouldn't keep me from having a good date with Bobby."

Laura shrugged. "Sure. But how're you going to write a novel with Evan Donaldson?"

Their conversation had come full circle, and Paige hadn't realized what Laura was implying until she said it outright. She buried her head in her hands.

"I don't know," she groaned. "Maybe we'll each write our own separate parts and Daisey will put them together." Even as she said it, she knew it wasn't true. Writing that way wouldn't result in a cohesive piece.

"For your sake, I hope you're ready for some spicy scenes, because Donaldson burns my mouth, and that's hard to do."

Paige groaned again. "This is going to be a disaster."

She felt Laura's hand on her arm, and she lifted her head. Laura patted her hand.

"It'll be okay. Just keep an open mind."

Paige doubted she could act unaffected by the steamy scenes Evan had promised to deliver, but she could try to see them from a different perspective. The characters weren't real, so whatever Evan had them do would only be in his imagination. She hoped her rationalization would be enough to keep her objectivity through the process.

Laura put her hands back on her hips. "Now, you go make plans with Bobby, and I'll make more of my afternoon orders."

"No promises," Paige called over her shoulder.

Chapter 5

Paige made plans to see Bobby on Saturday night.

She flurried around her house, fixing the flowers in a vase and then rushing to make her bed. It made her feel better to do the small tasks, as her anxiety had caused a lot of nervous energy to surface.

Paige hadn't been on a date since her divorce, and she was uncertain about the protocol. *Would she need to kiss him at the end of the date if she wanted to see him again? Did men still expect a woman to have sex with them after three dates?*

Was Laura right about her? Was she a prude? She tried to think of a reason to argue the point, but she couldn't settle on one. She talked about sex while it was going on, but she didn't share her experiences beyond her sexual partner.

While she was pondering her issues, her phone rang. At first, she expected to see Bobby's name, even though they'd only texted, but Daisey's name appeared on her screen.

"Have you started meeting with the boys yet?" Daisey asked.

"No, Daisey. I've hardly had a moment to—"

"You need to start today," she said. "I'll set it up."

The call ended. Paige stared at the phone in her hand for almost a minute, wondering about the brevity of the conversation.

Daisey was a busy woman, and she often cut her off, but she usually waited for her to start a response before she made plans for her. She hadn't even asked if Paige had other plans.

"Of course I don't have plans," Paige said out loud. She smiled when she remembered the date she'd scheduled for Saturday.

Within the hour, she received an email with a link to a meeting between Evan, Greg, and her. Daisey had scheduled it for later in the afternoon, but the time on the email only gave her two hours to prepare.

So much for writing down my ideas, she thought.

She tried to think about possible plots while she showered. She shaved her legs, even though they'd only see her from the neck up, and she put on a nice dress. When it was time for the meeting, she was presentable, but she had nothing to contribute to the conversation.

After the pleasantries, Evan led the talk. He spoke about deadlines and word counts. For someone who wrote free-spirited erotic tales, he seemed regimented.

Paige saw an opportunity to speak, and she took it. "I agree with what you've stated, Evan, but what's the book about?"

Greg backed her up. "That's a good point."

Evan made sure they saw his exaggerated eye roll. "Two romance authors and a mystery author are writing a novel together. What do you think it's about?"

Greg's jaw clenched.

Paige intervened. "So, it's a romantic mystery. Got it. But what about the plot?"

Evan leaned back in his chair. He had chosen the cover of his last book as his backdrop, but when he moved, Paige could see a bookshelf and awards in the background.

"We could make it a murder mystery," he suggested.

"I can work with that," Greg piped up. "There was a murder in the town over from me."

"Boring," Evan said, drawing out the first syllable. "We need to take the readers away from reality, not make them upset."

"Readers like to read stories that are based on real events," Paige defended. "You didn't even ask him what kind of murder."

"I already know about it," Evan said. "The wife was fed up with her husband nagging at her, so when he complained about his dinner, she poisoned it."

"There's more to it," Greg said, leaning forward. The muscles in his shoulder grew more apparent. "Her husband had been sleeping with her sister for years, and now the detectives on the case suspect that the woman's husband and sister were sleeping together in the same house and threatening to kill the wife if she left or raised an alarm."

"I guess the sister was lucky she didn't eat the same plate of spaghetti," Evan joked.

Greg smiled. "It was strychnine on Buffalo chicken that killed him, but yeah, she was lucky. She skipped town after the wife was arrested, and the police can't find her."

"It sounds like a good story," Paige mused.

"Okay. We'll write the story of the strychnine chicken, but I'm going to add a little ménage à trois."

"I'd expect nothing less," Greg chuckled.

Evan checked his wrist. No watch sat on it, but Paige and Greg took it as a sign to speed up their meeting.

"Should we each write a sample part and meet again to discuss them?" Greg suggested.

"That's fine," Evan agreed.

Paige found her voice, but both men had to lean into their monitors to hear her. "I thought we could bring in some of our characters."

"Oh, no." Evan shook his head. "I'm not putting Cindy and Kelly in this story for that maniac" — he pointed to the place where Greg showed up on his screen — "to kill them off."

Greg stroked his beard. "I wouldn't dream of putting an end to your bisexual friends. They're quite entertaining."

Paige felt like she'd been jabbed. She knew Cindy and Kelly were fictitious, but she couldn't stand the thought of Greg fantasizing about them. She wanted him to think about her instead. As she often did, she thought about a way she and Greg could be left alone and imagined him professing his undying love to her.

Greg was speaking when she tuned back into the conversation. "I think Paige is right, but instead of making our characters the focus of the story, we could make them secondary characters. I mean, Detective Luca lives ten miles away from the county where the crime took place."

Evan took in a sharp breath. "I guess Kelly could travel to another club to dance. Girls in her profession travel to different clubs all the time."

Greg waggled his eyebrows. "Are you sure she wants to leave Cindy behind?"

"Cindy has a kid," Evan answered. "She's tied to one spot."

Greg's face fell. "Not necessarily. If she had a good support group—"

Evan laughed. "I think I'll give Kelly some new experiences. She's always wanted to be with two men at once."

Paige cringed and put her hand up. "Eww. Next subject, please."

Both men stared at her. *Was this what Laura had meant when she'd said Paige was a prude?* After all, they were only talking about fictional characters, and they had to share ideas to write the book together."

"I'm sorry," she said. "I'm just not used to..." She couldn't finish her sentence, and the men were still staring at her.

"Haven't you ever thought about it?" Evan asked. He got the response he wanted when her eyes grew wide.

"No," she responded. "I'm a one-man-at-a-time kind of woman."

Evan grabbed his chin, pinching it lightly. "Really? Because Autumn has two men who go after her. I always assumed you wanted the same."

Paige felt her face redden. "Autumn and April are part of a lover's block. There are two women and two men, but the women can't figure out who would be their best partner."

"That only magnifies my point," Evan chuckled. He clasped his hands, making Paige feel like she was in his clutches. "Both women want both men, and—"

He went on explaining his logic, but Paige couldn't hear him over the blood marching through her ears. Greg's expression turned from amusement to pity, and he finally saved her.

"Hey, dude. I could sit here all evening and watch you make playful jabs at our innocent romance author, but I need to go. Can we talk about when we're going to meet next?"

Paige could hardly control her breathing, so she let the men talk. She put all her effort into bringing her body back into a relaxed state.

"I'm free on Saturday," Greg suggested.

Evan laughed. "Loser." He flipped something open on his desk that Paige guessed was a planner. "I'm busy that night, obviously" — he ran a hand over the top part of his body to exemplify his irresistibility — "but I can meet at six o'clock."

The boys had almost solidified the plans when Paige spoke up. "I can't meet on Saturday."

Evan raised his eyebrows. "Are you getting laid?"

Paige wanted to be disgusted, but she showed a look of indifference. "It's a first date, so no."

Evan snickered. "If I had a nickel for every time a girl thought that way about me, I'd be rich."

Paige saw an opportunity to make the situation lighter, and she took it. "Well, the date isn't with you, Evan, and I think you already have your entertainment planned for that evening."

He appraised her thoughtfully. "Right you are." He glanced at his planner again. "How about Sunday then? We could meet at two o'clock, in case Paige changes her mind about giving it up on the first date."

Paige put on her best smile and ignored his comment about her. They set the meeting for Sunday and went back to their lives.

Paige sat at her desk, her laptop's cursor blinking at her. If she was honest with herself, the project Daisey proposed had given her some wiggle room.

She'd never admit it to anyone, but Paige had experienced writer's block over the last month. She wasn't running out of ideas, but the stress in her life had shifted her focus from creativity to self-preservation.

She glanced at the letter on the counter. She'd have to take it to Sheriff Murphy sooner or later, but she didn't feel like bringing the memories to the surface again. The divorce had been hard enough, but dealing with the constant harassment was tearing her apart.

She gave up writing and bounced onto the couch. She could have slept on her pillow top mattress, but she'd avoided the room for months. It made her feel trapped, while the living room had several escape points, depending on how an intruder attacked her.

Paige had never considered how many doors and windows were in a room until her terrible experience. She had a good reason for preparing for the worst, as no one was protecting her.

She flipped through her phone. If she couldn't write, she could engage some readers on social media. She commented on a few of her favorite readers' profiles or pages and checked on her fellow writers.

Evan was up to no good, as usual. His latest picture showed him outside an abandoned amusement park with two women. The caption read: Are they a real-life Cindy and Kelly? I'm about to find out.

"I bet you are," Paige spoke, but she liked the post.

Evan had made the same comment about hundreds of women. He was with a new set every night, presumably sleeping with both of them. He claimed that none of the women matched his fantasies about Cindy and Kelly, though.

Paige believed the posts he made constantly were an attempt to unnerve Daisey. He wanted to hurt her because she wouldn't let him see Petal, but she used his lifestyle against him in court, reducing his visitation with Petal to the bare minimum. His efforts had been counterproductive, but since Daisey had taken so much from him, he assumed she could do nothing more, and he increased the frequency of his posts. The one Paige had liked was the third one that day.

Paige couldn't imagine sleeping with six people in one day. She hadn't had sex with six people in her life! Of course, no one knew that except for her ex-husband.

Paige decided she was going to be more open about sexuality. She may not discuss her own desires publicly, but she could be more receptive as other people talked about their experiences.

She looked at Greg's profile and noticed a new post. Her heart dropped into her stomach when she saw the picture included the three of them on a conference call.

As always, even though he had been speaking at the time he had snapped the photo, Evan looked dashingly handsome. Greg seemed collectively cool, and Paige was attentive. She wasn't smiling, but the blush on her face brought out her bottle-green eyes.

Paige guessed Greg had taken the picture while she was doing her best to avoid Evan's comments about sex. She liked the picture and read the caption. Greg stated his excitement about their new project and promised to keep his fans updated.

Paige didn't comment on the post. She looked at the picture for a long time, staring at the awkward moment.

After several minutes of battling her thoughts and feelings, she walked back to her desk. Once her fingers hit the keys, they came to life. She didn't stop writing for two hours. Just as one thought made its way onto her screen, another one followed it.

She went to bed feeling satisfied with her work. Her progress made her feel freer than she'd ever felt.

She couldn't wait to see Evan and Greg's jaws drop when they read it.

Chapter 6

"Just bump into her," Paige directed.

"But I'll spill the drinks on her," the man argued.

"That's the idea, Mark," the woman said. "She wants it to be like when we first met."

Mark nodded. "Oh, right. But didn't I spill coffee on you?"

Paige handed him the tray of sodas. "We don't want any first-degree burns if we can help it."

The woman, Karen, started walking down the sidewalk with a newspaper in her hand. Her view wasn't completely obstructed, but she did a good job of acting oblivious to the man approaching her.

Mark juggled the drinks a little too obviously, spilling them on Karen. He apologized right away, wiping his hands down her soaked top as he tried to clean up the disaster.

They conversed for a moment, Mark looking guilty and embarrassed and Karen annoyed but smiling, until Mark asked her to a movie. Karen accepted, and they walked out of the shot.

Paige turned off her camera. "That was fantastic, guys." She surveyed the wet spot gathering down the front of Karen's shirt. "I think we got it in one shot, and it's a good thing because I don't think it would be as believable if Karen was already soaked."

The couple laughed along with her joke. Several people who'd stopped to watch as they filmed dispersed.

"When do you think it'll go up?" Karen asked.

Paige tapped her camera. "I'll do some light editing, and the video will be up by Monday."

Mark smiled at his wife. "That's the week we met. Thanksgiving week."

They'd been married for fifteen years and had two children, but they still glowed when they looked at each other. Without saying a word, Paige snapped the moment on her phone camera. The picture of Mark and Karen at the end of the video would be a nice touch.

Paige walked back to her house, feeling in high spirits. The November air was unusually warm, but the wind through the fallen leaves announced the weather to come.

When she first established her presence as an author on social media, Paige was concerned that she wouldn't have followers. She arranged giveaways and made trendy posts, but nothing seemed to engage her readers. Then it hit her.

The readers who enjoyed her books the most were the people who liked "meet cutes" and sappy romances. She drew on that idea until she found her niche.

She posted one couple's story a month. She organized it in the same way as Mark and Karen's story, where the couple meets in an endearing way. Paige filmed couples who had just started dating and older people who had just shared their fiftieth anniversaries.

It showed Paige the type of romance she wanted. It had also helped her file divorce papers.

***

She edited the clip and posted it that night. It had been easy to do, as the segment was brief and she wasn't looking for perfection.

She checked social media, but she didn't see anything noteworthy. She silenced her phone and tried to go to sleep early.

She'd written her contribution to the new project in a fervor, never stopping to look at what she'd written. After her burst of creativity was over, she had several directions she could go with her part of the story, but she needed to see where her fellow authors stood with their offerings.

Why didn't we decide to outline it? she thought to herself. *It would have made everything so much easier, and I could have worked at my own pace.*

Her phone pulsed twice, indicating a text message. It wasn't really late, but most people didn't message her after nine o'clock.

She turned over and grabbed it from the end table. She was relieved when she saw it was from Bobby, as it meant her dad was fine, but a jolt of panic went through her when she thought about reading it. *Why did he need to talk to her so late?*

She glanced at the preview of the message. If she didn't officially open it, and it contained something she could leave until the morning, then she could claim that she'd been asleep when he'd sent the text.

The message was sweet, telling Paige how he thought of her and asking about her favorite restaurants. She decided it was harmless. She didn't acknowledge his compliments, but she responded to his question.

Bobby sent back a smiling emoji and told her he was looking forward to their date.

"That makes one of us," she said.

After she'd spoken, she realized it was true. Even though Bobby was attractive and nice, she didn't want to go out with him. There was nothing he could do to convince her it was a good idea, but she had obligated herself to the date, so she had to go through with it.

She returned his sentiment with a smiling emoji, hoping their conversation would end for the night. After he saw her message, three dots appeared on her screen, indicating he was typing a response. She breathed out a heavy sigh, but then the dots disappeared.

Thankful that he'd given up on their exchange, Paige returned her phone to the end table and reclined on the couch. She should have wondered if Bobby was having second thoughts about their date, as she hadn't returned his enthusiasm, but she didn't care. It would be a relief if he canceled it.

Chapter 7

On Friday, Paige had nothing to do. She could have been writing one of her own projects, but she'd hit a bump in her storyline, and the projection of her project with Greg and Evan would determine the direction she'd go.

She looked at the gray skies and turned her lip out over the plummeting temperature. Meteorologists expected the first snow of the season that evening, and it didn't thrill her. As a child, she'd loved the idea of snow, but as an adult, she was no longer crazy about it. The fluffy white stuff didn't get her out of class or provide conditions that kept her and her friends from playing for hours. That stopped when she went to college. The university she'd attended rarely canceled classes for inclement weather, and that meant that she had been driving in unsafe conditions and trudging across a slushy campus for three winters before she'd obtained her technical writing degree.

Spontaneously, she visited her father. He lived at the far end of town and up a rocky road that tested her car's transmission.

Paige rarely called ahead when she visited, as he was always happy to see her. When his house came into view, she noticed a white SUV parked next to his blue pickup truck, and she wondered who was visiting him.

As she passed the car, she noted the fake flowers on the dash and the air freshener dangling from the mirror. It wasn't from a discount store, as the scent was specific to a store frequented by middle-aged women.

Maybe one of her dad's friends had borrowed his wife's car to run errands. She heard female giggling when she climbed the steps, and she doubted she was right.

At the sound of another woman, Paige turned on her heels and headed back down the porch steps. She was almost at her car when the call of her name stopped her.

Her father stood on the porch leaning his hand against the railing. He was too old to hurry down the steps, so Paige met him on the porch for a hug.

"What are you doing, princess?"

Paige glanced uncertainly at the house. "I was going to visit with you for a little while, but I heard your company."

"Heard?" His silver eyebrows peaked.

Paige blushed. "You know, when I was on the porch. I heard giggling."

A hearty chuckle traveled up from his chest. "That's just Patricia." He gently tugged Paige's arm. "Come on. You can meet her. I think the two of you have a lot in common."

She let her father lead her into his small A-frame log cabin. They entered the living room, with a loft resting above it. From her angle, Paige could see into the kitchen. "Patricia," her father said in the direction of the kitchen. "Paige is here."

The woman breezed down the hallway, and when Paige saw her, her chin dropped. Patricia stood several inches above Paige's average height. Her blue eyes were almost crystalline, and her long nose and high cheekbones made her appear regal. She smiled with a bow-shaped mouth and extended her hand.

"Hello, Paige. Your father calls me Patricia, but you can call me Trish."

Paige shook her hand automatically as she took in her father's new girlfriend. Her father had always liked younger women, but this one was as close to Paige's twenty-eight years as any other woman he'd dated. No wonder he thought they'd have a lot in common.

They settled in the living room, amid her father's country-western decorations. Trish joined him on the loveseat, placing a hand on his thigh, and Paige took the leather recliner across from them.

Her father was in his seventies, but his mind was sharp. His body had rounded out from his days on the couch, but the weight had filled in the cheeks that had always seemed too thin, giving him a younger appearance.

Trish seemed nice, but Paige wondered about her motives for dating a man who was more than twice her age. She watched her carefully through their afternoon together, looking for any signs of a gold digger.

"You're as pretty as your father described you," Trish said. "You must share the conditioner you use with me. Your hair is gorgeous."

Paige was skeptical about compliments from strangers, but she shared the name of the product. To continue their talk, Paige asked Trish about her eyes.

Trish touched her fingers just under her eyes. "It must be an inherited trait. My mother has them, and my daughter does, too."

"How old is your daughter?" Paige asked.

Her father and Trish shared a look. Her father nodded and spoke on her behalf.

"When Patricia was a young teenager, she was forced to give up her baby. The adoptive parents sent her pictures because they knew she had wanted to keep her baby, but by the time Patricia was old enough to leave her parents' home, the couple had moved the child out of the country."

"They're missionary workers," Trish added, her voice thick with emotion. "She's had a good life." She stared down at her hands. "Better than the one I could have given her."

Paige had more questions, but the light-hearted visit had taken a sad turn, so she stared at her father for help. He took the hint and launched into a description of the adventures he'd shared with Trish in the short time he'd known her. When they told her about their trip to Dollywood, Paige's mouth turned down in the corners. That had always been a special place for her and her father.

Jimmy Turner had dated an array of women while Paige was growing up, but he'd always made time to share experiences with Paige. She had always felt like she was the most important woman in his life, and they'd had the most fun at theme parks. They shared a love of thrill rides, and most of their other day trips involved swinging bridges and monster trucks.

She pushed down her jealousy and tried to get to know Trish better. The woman seemed guarded about her family, but she opened up about her retail job.

"I work at the perfume counter," she told Paige.

Paige's eyebrows drew together. "Then how did you meet my dad?"

They shared a smile, and Paige sensed a deep connection. She was relieved that the woman didn't seem to be rooting around her father's money.

Her father held Trish's hand as he recounted their meeting. "I had been at the mall looking at some of the smelly soap you like, when I felt dizzy. The first chair I saw was in front of Patricia's counter, so I sat down. She called the EMTs and talked to me until they got there."

Paige was suddenly alarmed. "You had another episode with your heart?"

He waved away her concern. "It was just a small one." He brought Trish's fingers to his mouth and kissed them. 'Since then, I've had this lady to nurse me through any complications."

Her concern about the potential for gold-digging returned. Trish might think her father's heart condition made him an easy mark.

"What about you, Paige?" Trish asked. "Your father told me you were a writer. Do you have any new books coming out?"

"Actually, I just started a project with Greg Salem and Evan Donaldson."

Her father leaned up in his seat. "Doesn't Donaldson write smut?"

"Yes," Paige answered carefully, "but he always has a strong plot, and his characters—"

"You don't read that filth, do you, princess?"

As much as she didn't want to disappoint her father, Paige knew she had to tell the truth. "I read the books my colleagues put out, and they read my work, too."

Her father's stare hardened. "A man like that shouldn't be allowed around women."

Her father enjoyed reading, but he liked western novels. When he discovered Paige liked to read, he bought her books about the Oregon Trail. She wasn't really interested in them, but she read them to strengthen her bond with her father.

A thought occurred to her. "When did you read his work, Dad?"

"I don't have to read it," he said. "All the women talk about it."

Trish squirmed in her seat at the mention of other women. Paige's father liked to fish in every pond, so to speak, and he had known a lot of women in his seventy years. It was the reason his only wife, Paige's mother, had filed for divorce when Paige went to college.

Paige tried to make Trish feel more comfortable. "Have you read it, Trish?"

Trish seemed startled to be brought into their conversation. "I don't really read, but my friends at work like Evan Donaldson's books. I was always more interested in his failed romance with Daisey Flowers."

Her publisher's name was really Daisey Sams, but most people just used the name of her business when they referenced her. Paige had grown used to it.

"They made quite a stir."

Trish leaned forward, her eyes bright. "Why does he stay with her company? He could go anywhere he wanted, and any publisher would snatch him up."

Paige shifted uncomfortably. "I guess he stays because he has to finish up a ten-year contract."

"Ten years?" Trish sucked in a breath. "I've never heard of a contract that ran that long."

Paige smiled in return. She wasn't going to tell Trish that Evan had blindly signed the contract when Daisey had pushed it in front of him. He had trusted her explicitly, and Daisey knew it. When she discovered he was cheating on her, Daisey hurt him financially.

Trish was right about the top publishing companies. They all wanted him, but Evan was tied to Daisey Flowers Publications. If Daisey released him, Evan's books would become movies, but she held onto him, punishing him for breaking her heart.

"He deserves it," her father said.

Paige and Trish looked at him.

He threw up his hands. "What? The man's a cad!"

Trish giggled. "What is a *cad* exactly?"

He looked from Paige to Trish. "Women don't recognize a scoundrel when they see one. He puts up pictures of the women he's been with and runs through them like water."

"Sounds like someone else I know." Paige had spoken before she considered Trish, and she put her hand to her mouth.

Trish waved away her apology when she tried to express it. "I'm well aware of what I'm getting myself into. At least Jim has spent more than one night with me." She curled her fingers into his hand. "And I've felt his compassion for me."

Her father cleared his throat. "Promise me that you won't be another one of Donaldson's numbers, princess."

Paige promised. It was hard enough to be in the same room with Trish, who considered herself to be another one of Jimmy Turner's disposable girlfriends. She never wanted to feel the hurt she saw clouding Trish's eyes.

Chapter 8

Paige heard the doorbell ring as soon as she put the finishing touches on her eyeliner. Surveying the dance of freckles across her nose and the scar on her right cheek, she had decided not to put on concealer.

"He'll see me with my flaws and all," she said aloud before she jogged to the door.

When she opened the door, Bobby stared up at her. "You're gorgeous."

Paige blushed. He had dressed in a casual suit, but the tails on the jacket were long, hinting at a personal preference for classic attire. She searched for a proper compliment for him and decided against it. She didn't want to say something lame, like *your hair looks really shiny* or *your teeth match your shirt*, so she simply invited him inside.

"I don't think I should step inside your house yet."

Paige smiled at the old-fashioned sentiment. Her father would be pleased with her new suitor.

He offered her purple tulips, and she put one to her nose. She hadn't received many bouquets, so she hoped she was acting the way most women responded when their dates handed flowers to them. She put the tulips in water as Bobby waited at her door.

He guided her to his mid-sized luxury car, and she adjusted her coat before she strapped her seatbelt across her chest. To her dismay, Bobby didn't wear his seatbelt.

Bobby drove to Johnson City, a slightly bigger place than the town in which they lived. Paige was pleased with the restaurant he chose, as it was one of her favorites, and he requested a quiet booth, which she preferred over the section where they generally placed couples without children.

A little girl was playing with the straw in her cup, and she flipped it onto their table. Bobby was a little annoyed, but the child's mother apologized until Paige felt sorry for her.

The little girl turned around, sticking her tongue out at them. Paige smiled at her, and the little girl went back to eating.

"She's a little bratty," Bobby commented.

Paige leaned back, putting her napkin in her lap. "Oh, I don't think so. She's just spirited."

"Do you like children?" he asked.

She thought about it. "I guess so. I don't volunteer with youth services or anything, but they can be cute in small doses."

Bobby nodded along. "Do you see yourself having children one day?"

Paige cringed. The idea of pregnancy scared her more than the thought of labor and delivery. To her, a baby seemed parasitic, living off its mother for nine months. It wasn't a popular opinion, so she gave a safe answer.

"I don't know. Maybe one day."

The server approached the table and delivered the wine. Bobby stopped him as he walked away.

"We're ready to order."

Paige hadn't even glanced at a menu, so Bobby's enthusiasm perturbed her. She opened her menu to glance over it, and Bobby placed his hand over it.

"I looked over the selections before I picked you up. I can order for both of us."

Paige didn't want to spoil their time, but he was already ordering before she could protest. She listened to his choices, and it surprised her when he ordered meatless entrees. When the server walked away, she asked him about it.

He shrugged. "I'm not into meat. I hope you don't mind."

"I'm a vegetarian," Paige told him.

He seemed pleased, and they discussed their reasons for their lifestyle choice.

"I don't want to hurt animals," he told her.

Paige tore off a bite of bread but held it until she finished speaking. "That's commendable. I'm afraid my reason is a little more selfish. It bothers my stomach when I eat meat."

"So, can you eat eggs?"

She shook her head. "I haven't had an egg by itself since I was four."

A sly smile inched across his face. "That might make it hard to cook you breakfast in the morning."

Paige threw the piece of bread in her hand at him. "You're funny."

He took a sip of his wine and put his glass close to hers. "It's one of my many qualities. I can tell you more about my other ones if you let me."

Paige stared down at her plate, a blush creeping up her neck. *This is your chance,* she thought. *Prove that you're not a prude.*

Bobby came over to her side of the booth. Instead of being playful, he seemed concerned and a little guilty.

"I'm sorry, Paige. You don't know me well yet, but I like to play around a lot. I didn't mean to embarrass you."

Paige sat up straighter. "I'm not embarrassed at all." She wanted to say something more to prove her point, but their food arrived and saved her from an explanation.

Bobby didn't move, sitting beside her as they ate their meals. It made the conversation harder, but he seemed happier with their proximity to one another than he was with carrying on a conversation with her.

Paige preferred to sit across from her dates as they ate, but she didn't make a remark about his closeness. It would have been rude after he had moved to comfort her.

After their meal, they sipped more wine, but Paige didn't order a dessert. When she declined the signature cake, Bobby seemed hurt.

"Aren't you having a good time?" he asked after he sent the server away with his debit card.

"I'm having fun," Paige told him. "I'm just full from the meal. You ordered some really great food."

That seemed to brighten him. "They have cakes and doughnuts without chocolate, so if you change your mind, I can order one for us."

Paige's eyebrows came together. "When did I tell you I was allergic to chocolate?"

Bobby's eyes blinked a little faster than they had all night as he fumbled for an explanation. "I-I think it was earlier in the meal when we were talking about vegetarianism."

Paige let it go, but she had no recollection of telling Bobby about her allergies. She refused another glass of wine, mentally calculating whether her two glasses could have affected her memory.

When they got back into his car, shivering from the temperature, he pulled Paige to him. The console dug into her ribs, but she tried to enjoy the moment as he kissed her. His tongue moved too rapidly, and she gave up on trying to keep pace with him. Instead, she relaxed and concentrated on the motion of her lips.

The wine was still sweet on his tongue, and it intoxicated the kiss. If Bobby hadn't whipped his tongue from one side of her mouth to the other, Paige would have melted into him.

When he placed his hand on her breast, she allowed it. When he squeezed, she broke their contact.

He breathed heavily, his hand cupping the air. "Did I hurt you?"

"No. It's been a nice night, but I have a meeting tomorrow, so I need to go home."

He didn't try to talk her out of her decision until they made it back to their hometown. He put his arm over the back of her seat.

"Are you sure you don't want to have a drink at my house? I used to be a bartender, and I mix really great drinks."

She tried to think of a lie that wouldn't hurt his feelings. "I bet you do, but I need to have my wits about me in the morning. Six o'clock comes early."

"You have a meeting that early on a Sunday?"

Paige glanced out her window, happy to see her house in sight. "Yeah. It was the best time for all of us."

"Who is *all of us?*" he asked, air quoting her words with one hand.

She forgot that most men she knew didn't read, and she hadn't asked Bobby about his literary preferences, so he might not have been aware of her books. In fact, other than his brief mention of a past bartending job and his time as a chef, they hadn't talked about their work.

"I'm a writer," she told him, "and I'm putting together a book with Greg Salem and Evan Donaldson."

He nodded but offered no other response. He pulled into her driveway, and she waited as he rounded the car to open her door.

She pulled out her keys as they walked to her door. There was a tool on her keychain that helped her defend herself if someone tried to take liberties with her. It had been a present from her dad when she'd left her ex-husband. She didn't think she'd need to use it against Bobby, but she liked to be prepared.

She opened the door, and he gently twirled her around. "I'm not going to ask to come inside. You already told me you wanted to get some sleep before your meeting tomorrow." His hand glided down her chin. "But I want to leave you with something to make you think about me."

He kissed her deeply, forcing her to open her mouth a little wider. She was glad she didn't have a strong gag reflex, as Bobby pushed his tongue past the limits of most kisses.

He finally released her, smiling smugly as he walked away. He thought he'd done well. Even though it hadn't been a good kiss, it had certainly made an impression.

Chapter 9

Evan was in rare form, and he focused his playful energy on Paige.

"So, how was the date last night?" he asked.

Paige kept expression away from her features as she responded. "It was fine."

Evan winced. "Oh, he wasn't as good in the sack as you'd hoped?"

Paige tried to seem unaffected, but she could feel a muscle in her cheek twitch. "We never made it that far. I went home after dinner."

She was staring at Evan's part of the screen, but she could see Greg clearly. She may have imagined it, but she thought she saw a small smile.

"Poor sap," Evan went on. "Lucky for you that you didn't go home with someone who had the potential to strike out on the first date."

"You men and your baseball metaphors."

"It's America's favorite pastime," Greg chimed in.

Paige crossed her arms. "Well, I prefer football."

Both men guffawed. When they recovered, Evan spoke.

"Fine. Your date didn't score a touchdown."

Paige rolled her eyes. "Can we talk about something other than my sex life?" She saw the grin on Evan's face and added, "Or yours."

Evan faked a frown. "I guess we could talk about Greg's prospects."

Greg laughed. "What do you want to know?"

"Nothing," Paige answered for him. "As interesting as all this is, we need to get something done."

Without waiting for their response, she sent them the work she'd completed. "I sent an email with a portion of my story to both of you. You don't have to read it all, but it might help if you glanced over the first few paragraphs."

Evan's internet was the fastest, and he was scanning the pages as soon as she finished speaking. His eyes widened, and Greg's soon followed. Greg tried to mute his reaction, but he seemed contemplative.

"Well, well, well. Mr. Salem, it looks like we have a naughty girl in our presence after all."

Greg said nothing.

"Good for you, Paige. I didn't know you had it in you." Evan leaned back in his chair, rocking in it as he surveyed her.

Paige tried to gauge Greg's response, but he remained quiet. It was killing her not to know his reaction to her saucy scene.

Evan wasn't finished teasing her. "I mean, I've done all this" — he motioned to the part of the screen where he'd scanned her work — "but have you had as much fun as Robert did in your story?"

"It's not about me," Paige said.

"Sure it's not," Evan joked.

Greg cleared his throat. "I can see what you're trying to do, and I can respect it, but I don't think Daisey chose you as part of our group for you to write this way." He swallowed. "I think it will drive some of your regular readers away if they see one of your characters in this light."

Paige felt like Greg had stabbed her in the heart with an ice pick. "But I thought since Evan wrote about women, I could put something down from the male perspective—"

Evan stopped her by holding up a hand. "There are so many things wrong with what you just said. I don't try to write from a female perspective. I write my thoughts down, and I use female characters to tell the story."

Paige shook her head. "I hope you never say that publicly."

Evan's ego shined through. "I tell it to anyone who will listen."

Paige put her head in her hands. "And women still buy your books."

"What was that?" Evan asked.

Paige had no intention of repeating herself. "Can we just scratch what I sent you guys and talk about what we're going to do?"

They spoke about the plot and deadlines. A fresh idea came to Paige, and she suggested bringing in a quirky character to act as the murdering wife's best friend. She told them Robert could act as the friend's new beaux, and both men loved the change.

Evan held up his arm and stared at the imaginary watch on his wrist. "Well, it's time for me to go entertain two new beauties."

"Hey, Evan," Paige said before he left the meeting. "If you're the embodiment of Kelly and Cindy, how are you going to find two women who are like them?"

"I guess I'll have to find someone who is just like me." His answer was swift, and his screen went blank.

The square with Greg in it became larger, and the two of them sat side by side on her screen. Paige opened her mouth to announce her exit, but Greg interrupted her.

"I hope you aren't upset with me."

She blinked a couple of times before she answered. "I'm not upset."

He motioned with his finger. "You're doing that weird blinking thing you do when you're nervous or lying."

There was no way she was going to let Greg know he gave her butterflies. "I was a little hurt by your assessment of my contribution." It was the most professional way she could say it.

He nodded. "I knew it."

Paige rushed to defend her opinion. "You have a right to your opinion, but I'm trying hard to step away from the way people see me, and—"

"Why?"

His question took her completely off guard. She fidgeted, unsure about how to respond.

"I don't know. I was told I was a prude, and I wanted to prove that person wrong."

He stroked his beard before he moved closer to the screen. "Once again, why? Is one person's opinion worth sacrificing your professional brand?"

She shrugged her shoulders. "Part of me wanted to see if I could write something spicy."

"You certainly did."

She looked up at him, and his smile made her heart race. She was glad he couldn't see her fingers twisting off-screen.

"Pieces like that one should be saved for you to share privately," he went on. "You could give a sample to someone you're with, and what you wrote would definitely heat them up." He winked at her.

Paige had read somewhere that your stomach blushes when you blush. If that was true, her stomach was on fire. *Could Greg mean he was interested in her? Did he want to share intimate pieces of writing with her?* Her mind raced as she considered the possibilities.

He sat back in his chair. "Maybe the guy you dated last night could be the one to appreciate your skills in that area."

There was a sound off-screen, and Greg's attention went to something behind his monitor. He smiled apologetically and clicked out of the meeting.

It left Paige staring at a block that reflected a sad, slightly confused version of herself. She backed out and looked at the black screen for a long time, wondering if it was an omen of her doomed attempts at romance.

Chapter 10

"What I don't understand is why you haven't spoken a word about Bobby, but you've given me a play-by-play account of your conference call with Evan and Greg." Laura popped her arm with the clean dish towel she'd fished out from under the counter.

Paige shrugged. "It was more important to me to show that I could branch out as a writer than it was to talk about a desperately mediocre date."

She'd left out the part about trying to prove to Laura that she wasn't a prude. She doubted it would bother Laura that she had affected Paige, as that had been her obvious intention.

"He was that bad?"

Paige raised her eyebrows.

Laura rolled her eyes. "I mean, at dating. Did he open the door for you? Did he tip the staff at the restaurant well? Did he suck on a breath mint before he kissed you?"

"Yes to all, except the last one." Paige giggled. "I may have stolen the gum out of his mouth."

Laura humored her, but only a little. "You vanilla vixen!"

"Hey! I thought it was cute." She scrunched up her face. "And maybe a little disgusting."

"I'd steal anything out of Rob's mouth that he put in it," Laura said.

Paige shook her head. "Yeah, but you've been with him for seven years."

Laura considered her point. "That's true. But I had to start somewhere."

She set a pastry in front of Paige. "It's a crepe. Try it and tell me what you think."

Laura had a way of encouraging Paige to eat. Paige had gotten too thin over the past two years, but there were times she couldn't force a bite down her throat. Bread was her downfall, and Laura made it a point to place baked goods in front of her.

The crepes had been an option at the restaurant for a couple of months, and they were usually the first item to sell out daily. Paige knew it would be good before she tried it, and she savored every piece of the pastry as it passed her lips.

Laura cleared her plate and fork and refused the ten dollars Paige tried to hand to her. Paige was ready to leave when the bell over the door jingled.

The women turned expectantly, and a man in a long trench coat approached the counter. His stringy hair dangled around his face, and his hands were in his pockets.

Paige wasn't concerned until Laura gave her a pointed look. It was one of the rare times in the afternoon that the shop was without customers, so the man's controlled movements and the way he squinted at the muffins and doughnuts through the glass made the women uncomfortable.

He looked over, and his dark eyes landed on Paige. "You're the famous writer, right?"

It horrified Paige that he'd recognized her. She'd had a couple of crazed fans beg her for free books or to marry them, but this was the first time she'd felt like her life was in danger.

She decided to play it off. "Yes. Did you want me to autograph something for you?" She held up an unused napkin.

He sucked his tobacco-stained teeth. "Naw."

Paige didn't want to say anything more, as she feared it might trigger him. Laura moved to the register, where she kept a handgun under the counter. She had a permit to carry it, and she'd encouraged Paige to get one, too, but Paige was too scared of guns to buy one for protection. Laura's eyes were trained on the man's pockets as he was moving something inside one of them.

I don't want to die, Paige thought.

She thought about Laura. It would devastate Rob if something happened to his wife. No one would be upset about Paige's death, except for her parents.

I'll get his attention on me, she thought. *I'll find a way to get him outside, even if I have to flirt with him. Then Laura will be safe.*

"It's a nice—"

She stopped speaking when his hand moved out of his pocket. He placed the contents in front of Paige.

"Nate sends his regards," he said. "You haven't written him back, and my boy's dyin' in the pen without commissary money or a word from his wife. You're cold-hearted."

The man staggered out the door. The women were frozen in place until he was out of their sight. When he left, it felt like the room breathed with life again.

Laura grabbed her arm. "Are you okay? I thought I was going to have to shoot him."

"I was so scared," Paige admitted. "I haven't been that scared since—"

Laura stroked her arm. "I know."

She glanced down at the letter. "I have another one of these at home. I've been meaning to turn it in to Sherriff Murphy."

"He wrote you, and you didn't tell anyone?" Laura paced, putting her hand on her forehead. "You know they'll stop his outgoing letters if they find out he's writing to you. It's in the court order."

"He put another name above my address, but I thought they checked them before prisoners sent them out."

Laura used her hands as scales. "The people who check them can catch some things, but if he didn't use your name, and you didn't alert them to your address change, then there's nothing more they could do."

"Should I call the sheriff to come here, or should I take both letters to him?"

Laura's mouth formed a grim line. "I don't want the police here, Paige. Nothing happened, and it would drive away the customers."

"I understand. I'll go home and grab the other letter and go to the police station."

Laura's eyebrows climbed. "You're not leaving here alone. I'll call Rob to take you home."

Paige laughed. "I'm capable of walking three blocks to my house."

Laura grabbed her phone and quickly typed a text message. "Under normal circumstances, I'd agree with you, but after what happened, you're not leaving here without a big, strong man."

"Is there any way around it?"

"Yeah," Laura said. "You can leave with a big, strong woman."

Since her friend was unmovable, Paige waited until Rob arrived. They drove to her house, and she grabbed the other letter, making sure all the doors and windows were locked.

At the police station, Rob tapped his foot as they waited for the sheriff. "I've not done anything, but it makes me as nervous to be here as I was when I was sent to the principal's office." Rob flashed an uneven smile and put a muscular arm around her shoulders. "It'll be okay, though."

Paige couldn't tell if he was talking to her or himself. Rob wasn't usually apprehensive about anything. At least, he had never seemed that way.

"Paige," the sheriff said, extending a hand to Rob and bringing her in for a one-armed hug. "What brings you out here?"

Paige handed him the letters. "Nathan sent me a letter, but he put another woman's name on it."

Sheriff Murphy surveyed the letters, his salt-and-pepper eyebrows going up. "Did you move out of your dad's house? This isn't the—"

Paige interrupted him. "I moved out a couple of months ago. "I know I was supposed to send them my new address, but I thought if they had it, Nathan could somehow get it."

The sheriff scrutinized her. "I think you know better."

Paige's shoulders slumped. "I do, but my mind has been working crazily since he was finally arrested."

Sheriff Murphy stroked his mustache. "I don't doubt it. That monster doesn't deserve the air he—"

Rob stopped him before he got carried away. "Is there anything Paige can do now?"

The sheriff surveyed the letter. "There aren't any direct threats, but I can tell the warden what he's up to." He addressed Paige. "Since you didn't inform them when you moved, they won't do anything about these letters, but if you call them, they'll keep him from sending letters to your address, no matter who he puts on the envelope."

Paige's eyes filled with tears, and she turned her head. "He'll just find another way."

Her voice was barely above a whisper, but both men heard her. Rob patted her arm as Sheriff Murphy searched for her eyes.

"That letter" — Rob nodded to the one in Sheriff Murphy's other hand — "was hand-delivered. Some guy brought it to Laura's shop and scared the girls to death."

The sheriff examined the envelope. "I didn't notice that this one was missing a stamp. Who gave it to you?"

Paige gulped audibly. "Some guy with stringy hair and a trench coat."

Sheriff Murphy shook his head. "That could be any number of people."

"It seemed like he'd been close with Nathan," Paige recalled. "He said 'my boy, Nate', and Nathan never shortened his name when we were together."

"It's probably someone who was locked up in the pen with him," Rob said.

Sheriff Murphy agreed. "I'll ask for a list of men who've been released from that institution lately. I bet one of them will be the man who gave you this letter." He opened the envelope and thumbed the hand-written pages. "I don't know how he got this letter by the people at the penitentiary, but I'd be willing to bet they never saw it."

Rob took a page of the letter and scanned it. "This doesn't sound threatening to you?" He pointed at a line.

Sheriff Murphy leaned in but shook his head. "It doesn't mention direct physical harm. He could argue it."

Rob turned away from them and ran a hand through his hair. "So, Nathan is just going to keep finding ways—"

A sharp look from Sheriff Murphy stopped him. "Paige has a high profile, and she's staying in her hometown. Someone is always going to find her."

Paige had been internally debating selling her house, but Sheriff Murphy was right. She could move anywhere in Erwin, Tennessee, and Nathan would eventually find her.

The light was fading when Sheriff Murphy walked them out. "Why don't you stay with your friends tonight?"

Paige declined. "I want to stay in my own house. Nathan's in jail, so he can't hurt me."

"What about your dad's then? I'd feel more comfortable if you were somewhere safe while I figure out who the fellow is that gave you this letter." He held it up.

"I'm safe at home," Paige argued.

"He means somewhere with a gun," Rob said. "Laura and I both have one, and your dad has an arsenal."

"I'm fine," Paige affirmed.

The sheriff and Rob exchanged a glance. "See if you can talk some sense into her," Sheriff Murphy told Rob as he hugged Paige. "I'll make the calls, and that boy will have to stop harassing you."

Paige was certain of one thing. Nathan was never going to give up.

Chapter 11

Paige was disappointed in herself for letting Rob talk her into spending the night with them. She felt like a huge inconvenience.

Laura and Rob lived in a one-bedroom apartment within walking distance of the shop. The apartment was small, but it was perfect for them, as they were hardly ever there. They had basic furniture, but no decorations adorned the vanilla walls, and the shades stayed closed, as they both left before sunrise.

Laura and Rob had tried to encourage Paige to sleep in their bed, but she had flatly refused. They put blankets on the couch, and even though it was comfortable, Paige missed the chaise lounge attached to her sectional sofa.

Laura brought her a glass of wine and sat on the other end of the couch. "I'm glad you decided to stay."

"I feel like an imposition."

"You're not," Rob called from the kitchen.

He'd been washing dishes since they'd gotten there. The apartment was mostly tidy, except for the dishes and laundry. With their schedules, neither Rob nor Laura had the time to take care of more than simple household chores.

"Do you want to talk about it?" Laura asked.

"You were there, too. Do you want to talk about it?"

Laura gulped her wine and set the glass on the coffee table. "Not really. I just want to follow my husband into our bedroom and let him wrap me in his strong arms."

Rob wandered into the living room, flexing one of his arms. "I'm ready when you are, babe."

Laura offered to stay up with Paige, but she told her she was too tired to carry on a conversation. It was a lie, and Paige listened to Laura and Rob as they talked in their room.

When the heat kicked on, it drowned their voices, but when it was mostly silent, she could hear snatches of their conversation. She trained her ears on it, thinking she heard her name.

"I told her for years..."

"I know, but..."

"...when she had the bruises at the Apple Festival..."

They seemed to be discussing her marriage to Nathan. She stopped listening and closed her eyes. After the next time the heat kicked off, she heard giggling and other sounds consistent with an activity she hadn't done in a while.

They weren't loud, but it was possible they were unaware of how sound carried through the apartment. Paige willed herself to go to sleep, and when she did, she fell into a dream where she was in her bed with a man's hands moving from her shoulders to her hips. She thought it might be Bobby, but the man's kisses were unrushed, and when she opened her eyes, she saw Greg's face.

***

Paige heard Rob and Laura leave for work, but she pretended to be asleep. When they were gone, she gathered her stuff and walked home.

The morning air was brisk, but she weathered it in the dark. It was the part of the morning that was almost daybreak, so it signaled night owls to sleep and early risers to get up and start their day. It felt safe, and Paige wasn't concerned until she had to pass Laura's shop. She thought Laura would be in the back, readying muffins and croissants, but she worried her friend would see her slip past the shop.

Paige rushed past the tall windows without glancing inside. She hoped the fading darkness covered her well enough.

She knew Laura would be upset with her for leaving without another person with her. Laura may have intended for either Rob or her to drive Paige home during their lunch break, but Paige had no intention of waiting there that long.

When she opened her door, something felt off, but a quick check around the house calmed her nerves. She tried to write, but her mind was too hazy from her brief sleep. She settled on a sitcom and sipped a bottle of water.

After the sun was high in the sky, Paige felt comfortable enough to lie down on the chaise lounge and go to sleep. The urgent pounding on the door was the next thing she heard.

***

Paige stumbled to the door and looked out the peephole. Recognizing the caller, she checked the mirror next to the door.

She looked almost frightening, with black streaks of mascara and eyeliner. She grabbed a baby wipe and cleaned her face while she sloshed mouthwash through her teeth. A second series of loud knocking started before she opened the door.

Lewis Novack stood on her porch, the lines in his forehead creased. "What took you so long to get to the door?"

The chilly breeze rushed into the doorway, even though the sun was bright, and Paige wrapped her arms around herself. "I was asleep. Do you want to come in?"

He stepped inside before she could move out of the way, and he brushed past her. He smelled the same as he did in high school, musky and warm, and nothing about his appearance was out of place. From his rigidly starched police uniform to his perfect blond hair, Lewis Novack was still the best-looking ex-boyfriend Paige had ever had.

Lewis got right to the point. "The guy who gave you Nathan's letter was Willie James."

Paige's stomach dropped, and she sat down on the couch. Lewis joined her, picking up both her hands.

"The sheriff and I went out to Willie's trailer this morning, but his girlfriend, Caroline, said he was gone." He narrowed his blue eyes. "He was there, though, and we knew it, so the sheriff explained very loudly that you'd press charges if he approached you again."

Paige leaned into him, and Lewis's arms circled her. They stayed wrapped together for a moment before he spoke again.

"I don't think he'll bother you again, but I get off work in a couple of hours, and I can drop back by your house." He paused before he added, "If you want me to."

At that moment, Paige wanted nothing more than for Lewis to stay. She remembered the fun they'd had, and after all the stress she'd been feeling, she would have loved to have had Lewis back in her bed.

Lewis was safe. He wasn't good at monogamy, but he was better than a super-hero if a woman needed his help. Paige was sure he'd spend every night with her until she resolved her current problem with Nathan. Then he'd drift away, just like he had two other times in her life.

"I'm okay," she told him. "I have Laura, and I'll go stay at her apartment again if I need to."

He bounced the palm of his hand off his head. "I should have thought about that. I got worried when you didn't answer the door, and I thought about break-ing it in. It should've occurred to me you could have stayed somewhere else last night, like with your dad, a friend, or a boyfriend." His eyebrows shot up when he mentioned a boyfriend.

"No boyfriend," Paige assured him, but she felt guilty when she thought about Bobby. She'd only gone on one date with him, so she doubted Bobby thought of her as his girlfriend.

"We could remedy that." Lewis leaned in for a kiss.

Paige backed away, placing a hand on his police vest. "We both already know how that ends."

Lewis looked at the floor. "After Patti left, I've tried to turn over a new leaf, but no one believes I've changed." He looked up at Paige, and when she saw the starbursts in his beautiful blue eyes, she almost took him up on his offer.

He pecked her lips. "Take care of yourself, Paige. I'll check on you." She raised her eyebrows, and he amended, "When I'm on duty."

He strutted to the door, locked it, and pointed to the deadbolt before he went out. Paige got up after he shut the door and slipped the deadbolt into place.

She watched Lewis from her window at an angle where he couldn't see her. "I should've told him to stay."

She sighed and grabbed her laptop. Inspiration suddenly gripped her, and she'd written almost thirty pages of manuscript before the effects of Lewis's visit wore off.

Chapter 12

Pounding on her door jolted her awake. She blinked twice, trying to adjust to the early afternoon sun pouring through the windows.

"Princess!" her father yelled.

Paige hurried to the door, opening it wide. Laura and her father stood on the porch.

"You didn't answer your phone," Laura said, tears brimming her eyes. "I didn't know what to do. I called the police, and Lewis told me he'd been here, but—"

"Lewis Novack!" Her father's voice demanded attention. He brushed past Paige to scout her apartment.

"What's that about?" Laura whispered.

Paige pulled her inside. "He was my first boyfriend."

Laura's chin dropped. "It looks like we have something in common. He wasn't my first," she amended, "but he was one of the many before I found Rob."

"Don't say his name around my dad," Paige whispered. When she heard him in her back bedroom, she confided in her friend. "He caught him in my bed."

Laura's hands went to her mouth. "That explains a lot."

Paige drew her eyebrows together. "What do you mean?"

"One of your first sexual experiences was witnessed by your dad. That would stifle some sexual expression."

Paige's father entered the room. "He's gone."

"He only stayed about five minutes, and we didn't go past the living room couch." Her words didn't seem to ease her father, so she went on. "He was on duty. Nothing happened."

"That boy has a reputation."

Paige and Laura looked at each other.

Paige tried again. "Dad, Lewis is a grown man, and he's trying to change."

Her dad's finger flew up. "He better not be messin' with you again. I swear, that boy has his fingers in every honeypot in the county. He was with that girl who couldn't remember who she was, and he flies back and forth between Patti and whoever he's got on the line."

By the time he was finished, both women were trying to keep from laughing. Laura tried to appease him.

"Mr. Turner, I have to go. Paige said she's not with Lewis Novack, and no crazy person has tried to kill her, so we should probably get going. Rob's lunch break will be over soon, and—"

"All right, all right." He put his palms up. "I know when I'm not wanted."

Paige rushed to hug him. "I always love when you visit me, Dad, but I have litter-box breath, and I'm in desperate need of a shower."

Her friend and father left, and Paige grabbed a couple of toaster pastries. While she waited for them to pop up, she glanced through her phone. She hardly looked at the calls and messages from Rob, Laura, and her father, but she had two messages from Greg and one text from Bobby.

Her heart leaped when she clicked on Greg's messages, but her spirits fell when she saw it was a response to the pages she'd sent him to review and a reminder about their upcoming meeting. Bobby's text spoke of her beauty, and he asked her to another dinner.

She called Booby, still completely dispirited over Greg's professional messages. No matter how much she wanted Greg to like her, he held her at arm's length, flirting with her just enough to get her hopes up, and then making her feel like she meant nothing to him. If it hadn't been for the night they'd met in person, her feelings never would have gotten that far. But that was months ago, and she needed to find a way to move on.

Bobby answered on the third ring. "Hey, beautiful lady! Do I get to take you to dinner tonight?"

"No," Paige said. "But you can cook for me. What's your address?"

***

Paige dressed in her short navy-blue dress with the long V in the front. She used a strapless bra to give her breasts a better shape and threw a faux fur coat over her shoulders.

Bobby offered to pick her up, but Paige opted to drive to his house. He lived in a two-story colonial on the south side of town. She'd passed some run-down buildings to get to it, but his house was well-maintained.

His eyes popped when he helped her out of her coat. "You look gorgeous." He looked down at his white crewneck and tan pants. "I feel underdressed."

If anyone felt underdressed, it was Paige. She shivered and rubbed her hands together as she followed her host. Luckily, the kitchen was warmer, full of residual heat from the oven and warm smells from the food Bobby had laid on the table.

"Don't worry about the turkey," he said when he noticed her staring at the bird-shaped protein. "It's really tofu."

They sat at the table, and Paige enjoyed everything Bobby had prepared. The rolls were buttery and light, the mashed potatoes were fluffy and perfectly seasoned, and the tofu was just crispy enough to delight her tastebuds.

After the meal, Bobby pulled out a homemade cheesecake. It was slightly brown on top, but the hint of sour cream lingered with every bite. It was subtle but tasteful.

"Everything was so delicious," she told him. "I know why you're a chef."

"I may have fibbed a little," he admitted. "I'm only a food worker, but I'm in a distinguished kitchen, so I have room to move up in my field."

"A little white lie doesn't hurt anything," Paige said. "Especially when you can make food like this."

"I could cook for you every night," he said, pouring more wine into her glass.

Paige had drunk three glasses of wine, and even with the food, she felt a strong buzz. "I shouldn't drink anymore. I have to drive home."

Bobby moved his chair close to hers and put his hand on her thigh. "You don't have to go home. You could stay here."

He kissed her, and the wine helped her look past the speed of his tongue in her mouth. He picked her up and carried her to the couch.

After an intense make-out session that went on much longer than Paige had initially intended, Bobby moved off her body. "Either I'm going to have to call a driver for you, or I'm going to carry you to my bed. It's your choice."

It took a matter of seconds for a battle to rage through Paige's mind. On one hand, she hadn't known Bobby for long, but on the other hand, he was kind and sweet enough that he went to all the trouble to prepare a fantastic dinner for her. He seemed safe, and unlike Lewis, she had more of a possibility of a future with him.

"I can walk," she decided.

His forehead creased. "To your house?"

A laugh erupted from her chest. "No, silly. I can walk to your room." She put on her best bedroom eyes.

He tried to control it, but surprise crossed Bobby's features. "Okay, then. Let me just fix up my room a little."

She traced a swirling line down his chest. "I'll meet you up there."

"Five minutes," he told her but amended it after their next kiss. "Three. I only need three minutes."

"I hope you mean to get ready," she teased.

"Yep," he responded, either unaware of her meaning or confident in his abilities. She hoped it was the latter.

Paige used the bathroom downstairs, but before she went upstairs, she thought about the condom in her purse. She didn't know if Bobby had protection, but she had remembered to bring some. She hadn't expected to have sex, but she tried to be prepared.

Bobby had known all the right things to say to her. They both liked reading and gardening. He had a stable job and a home, and when there was a pause in their conversation, he picked a new feature on her to compliment.

She opened the coat closet and pulled out her coat. He had placed her purse over the hanger, and she reached inside it. Then her heart stopped.

All six of her books were lined up on the floor of the closet. The pages were frayed, as if they'd been read often, and colored sticky notes peeked out from the pages.

When she reached down to pick up a book, Bobby called down. "Is everything okay?"

"I'll be up in a minute," she responded, hoping her voice didn't sound as unsure as she felt.

She opened the book, her debut novel, to the first note. It read: *May love tulips.* On the page, a sentence was underlined that detailed Autumn's first date with Robert. He had given her tulips.

She flipped to the next note. *Enjoys blueberry muffins.* Autumn had indulged in her favorite snack after her first breakup with Robert.

The note at the end was the worst. *May not want sex. Be firm.*

What was that supposed to mean? The notes were obviously correlating the character's actions with Paige's likes and wants, so did he mean that he'd force himself on her if she refused him?

It was all too much for Paige, and without alerting Bobby, she slipped on her coat, put her purse over her shoulder, and walked out.

She didn't trust herself to drive, so she called a driver. Aware that she was moving away from a situation, the driver responded quickly.

She was thankful that the estimated arrival time was less than five minutes. It was highly likely that she could flag them down before they made it to Bobby's address.

Bobby called her. At first, she ignored it, but after two rings, she answered her buzzing phone.

"What's going on, Paige? Why did you leave?"

"I found the books," she told him. "That's pretty creepy, Bobby."

There was a brief pause. "You're my favorite writer. Of course I have all your books."

"Why didn't you tell me you'd read my work?"

He breathed into the line. "It didn't really come up."

A car approached, but it wasn't her driver. She moved into the grass, and the older model vehicle pulled into the driveway behind her.

"What about when we were talking about our favorite authors and the books we'd read? Why couldn't you have told me then?"

"I didn't think you were this self-absorbed," he returned.

She stopped walking and stabbed the soft earth with her heel. Bobby was trying to shift the focus onto her, but unfortunately for him, she had a lot of experience with narcissistic men.

"I think you know it's not about the books. It's the notes you wrote about me. You were comparing me to my main character."

He was quiet, and Paige thought she'd see her driver before he spoke again. She wasn't giving up on her side of the argument. When he spoke again, Bobby wasn't as self-assured. If anything, he sounded manic.

"You need to realize that I'm your biggest fan. No one else could've read between the lines and seen the similarities between you and Autumn. You both have red hair and blue-green eyes, and she just got out of an abusive relationship—"

"Hey, I wrote that long before I had any trouble."

"That's not what Nate said."

Her blood turned to ice, and it had nothing to do with the temperature. "You were in jail with him, too?"

He chuckled, realizing that he'd regained the upper hand. "I've never been to jail, Paige, but I know how to get in touch with an inmate. You wouldn't believe how helpful they can be when you tell them you're dating their wife."

She doubted most people in the penal system would be accommodating under those circumstances. However, given Nathan's history, she wasn't surprised at his willingness to help someone who was as obviously crazy as him.

She backed up, her line of thinking jumped to the day they met. It had seemed natural, but had Nathan had a hand in it?

"Did you even take those muffins to your mom?"

"My mom's been dead since I was a kid," he told her. "I just wanted to have what you call a 'meet cute'."

Her mind swirled around her social media posts. Bobby had used her past relationships, social media, and books against her. It was everything she felt that defined her in her current stage of life.

Headlights washed over her, and without seeing the car or driver clearly, she knew it was the ride she'd reserved. She waved her hands, and the vehicle stopped. After showing the driver her license, he unlocked the doors for her.

"Look," she whispered, "we're through. I don't want to see or hear from you again. I'll pick up my car tomorrow."

She hung up and rested her head against the back of the seat. The effects of the wine had worn off, but she was more comfortable riding home than driving while she was seething with anger.

"Rough night?" her driver asked.

"You have no idea."

Chapter 13

Paige paced until her father called her. It had taken swallowing every ounce of her pride, but she'd asked her father and Rob to pick up her car from Bobby's house. Her father had told her he'd pick it up around one, but it was almost four o'clock, and no one had returned her worried messages with more than 'Everything's fine'.

Just after the turn of the hour, she heard two vehicles. When she looked out of her window, she spotted her dad's truck and Rob driving her car.

With a sigh of relief, she opened the door, welcoming the two men out of the cold. They kicked the dusty snow off their boots.

"I was about to call in the calvary," Paige said, adopting a phrase her dad had used.

She'd expected humor in return, but their expressions were dim. Rob kept looking at her father, waiting for him to speak.

Paige crossed her arms. "What happened? Did Bobby threaten you guys?"

Rob shook his head. "We never even saw him."

"The coward stayed in his house," her dad stormed. "He didn't even answer the door when the sheriff pounded on it."

Paige's hand went to her mouth. "Why did the sheriff need to be there?"

Her father turned around and paced from one end of the room to the other. He was angry, and when he was younger, a man like Bobby would have been beaten up for disrespectful actions. Rob saw Jim Turner couldn't master his temper and spoke for him.

"He slashed your tires," he said. "Your dad called the sheriff, but Bobby didn't come to the door. Since it was on his property, and he invited you there, you can press charges, but between you and me, he lives in a rough neighborhood, so he's gonna argue that one of his neighbors did it."

Her dad's face was as red as a tomato, but he rejoined the conversation. "I had your car towed and put new tires on it. The sheriff will be by later this evening to bring the papers for you to file charges."

Paige shook her head. "Nope. I'm done, Dad. I'll pay you back for the tires and tow truck fees, but I'm not going to court against Bobby. It's a small price to pay to be rid of him."

"You live in the same town, Paige," Rob said flatly.

Paige crossed her arms over her stomach. "I don't care. I managed not to meet him until a couple of weeks ago, so maybe I can stay away from him in the future."

"Laura can ban him from the shop," Rob argued, "but what about book signings?"

Paige laughed dryly. "I doubt that he's *my biggest fan*" — she mocked, putting up air quotes — "if he's slashed my tires. I don't think I'll have to worry about it."

"How do you find these guys?" her dad asked.

He was off in his own world. He had finally sat in the chair by the door and stared at a place on the blank wall.

His words stung Paige, and her voice was barely above a whisper when she answered him. "They seem to find me."

Rob tried to make a few jokes, comparing the situation to a popular country music song, but Paige and her father held their respective positions. There was nothing Rob could say to make the situation lighter.

"I'm going to go now," her father announced. He hugged Paige and stomped out the door.

Rob tried to console her after he walked out. "Your dad's just upset that he couldn't defend your honor."

"I know," Paige returned. "But he's right. I find the lowest scum of the world."

Rob gave her a one-armed hug. "Your dad's my ride, so I gotta go, but don't be hard on yourself. There's a lot of crappy guys in the world, and you happened to sleep with one last night."

Her eyes widened as she realized her father and Sheriff Murphy probably thought the same thing. "I didn't sleep with him. I was going to, but I found out he was a crazed fan, so I left."

He opened the door and waved to her father. "At least you dodged that bullet. I'm sure Laura will call you later about all this."

She thanked him, and Rob closed the door. She stood at her window for a long time, thinking about her father's words, and evaluating her feelings about them.

Her relationship with Nathan had been an utter failure. Paige had thought he had loved her, so when the beatings started, she'd made excuses for her bruises instead of leaving. She wasn't sure what Bobby had been talking about the previous night. She'd had a boyfriend who had cheated on her before she'd met Nathan, but no one had abused her before her husband.

A knock at the door jolted her. She peeked out the window at an angle, careful not to show herself.

It was Lewis. She couldn't believe the sheriff had sent him to her house again.

He breezed past her without an invitation and plopped on her couch. She shut the door and stood over him.

"Where are the papers?" she asked. "Wasn't I supposed to file charges?"

"Yeah," he said, eyeing her. "You know, when you turned me down the other night, I didn't know it was because you were seeing Bobby Fields."

Paige rolled her eyes. "It wasn't because of him." She motioned between them. "We aren't exactly good for each other, Lewis."

He hopped off the couch and caressed her face. "I don't remember that."

He leaned in to kiss her, but Paige backed away just enough to leave his hand holding air. "I don't think we should see each other."

He laughed good-naturedly. "Okay. I just had to try."

He strode to the door, talking as he grabbed the knob. "I'll be back with the paperwork."

"Don't worry about it."

She thought she saw a wounded look pass across his features before he covered it with a grin. "I know I came on a little strong, but—"

"It's not that," she said quickly. "I just don't think anything will happen to Bobby if I press charges."

"You're probably right, but he'll just do it again to the next girl who—"

"But she probably won't have any kind of fame."

Lewis's eyebrows went up. "I didn't think about that." He stroked his chin. "Do you think he's a fame-seeker?"

Paige shrugged. "I don't know. I thought I had a good idea about his character, but I was wrong."

Lewis raised his eyebrows and gave her a sideways smile. It was one of his cutest looks, but he had no idea it affected her.

"I'm going to talk to him," he said seriously. "You're not going to press charges, but I think I should make him think you are."

"Thank you, Lewis."

He held out his arms. "What about a hug before I go?"

She held out her hand. "I'll give you a friendly handshake."

"I think I'll pass," he returned with a wink.

***

Paige tried to go through her evening routine without thinking about the men in her life, but every time she thought she was free of them, a thought about Bobby, Lewis, or her father would pop up and anger her.

"How dare he jump to conclusions!" she yelled at her television. "My father knows I'm a grown woman. I can have sex if I want." She nodded, satisfied with her rant until she thought about it more deeply.

It had miffed Lewis that Bobby had been the recipient of her attention instead of him. He'd plopped onto her couch like he expected her to fall into his arms. The more she thought about it, the more she believed she was angrier with him than she was with Bobby for slashing her tires.

On the other hand, Bobby had deceived her. He studied her books, not because he wanted to learn more about her, but because he thought he could find a way for her to have sex with him.

"And I was going to," she admitted, crying into her hands.

She was going to sleep with Bobby because Laura believed she was a prude. She loved her friend, but Laura's remarks could sometimes cut her to the core.

Paige flicked off her television. She listened to the silence. It invaded her ears and threatened to take over her mind.

"I'm done."

How was she done? She didn't want to abandon her friends and family, but she needed space.

Before she could argue with herself, she grabbed a suitcase and threw some things inside it. She picked up her laptop and phone and went out the door.

Chapter 14

She was almost at the South Carolina line when her phone rang. She answered the call on the Bluetooth in her car.

"Where are you?" Greg asked.

She palmed her forehead. "I'm so sorry! I forgot about the meeting."

"Hold on a minute."

She heard some rustling and mumbling. She pulled over to the shoulder of the road while he was talking.

"I told Evan we'd meet with him tomorrow night," he explained when he rejoined their conversation.

"Thanks. I'm sure he'll be happy to get a jump on his evening."

Greg chuckled. "He already had. He had a woman sitting on each leg. There's no way we would've gotten any work done."

"I guess it was a good thing that I had a breakdown then." She laughed, but it fell flat.

"What happened?"

His voice was so warm and sincere that she found she wanted to tell him. She felt a little silly for doing it, but she explained everything that had happened to her over the past several days. She left out the part about Lewis, feeling as though she may have overreacted.

"Nathan and Bobby are real pieces of work," he said. "What do you plan to do?"

She sighed. "Right now, I'm borrowing a page out of my mother's book, and I'm running away."

"Oh, that sounds dangerous. Have you made any reservations?" He was steady and diplomatic.

"I don't really know where I'm going to go. I may end up in Myrtle Beach or Disney World."

"I vote for Disney World." His smile carried over the line. "I only live an hour away."

She considered her options a little more. "You know, Sea World and Universal Studios are in Orlando, too. Maybe it would be a good time to see them." His comment about living nearby made her feel brave, and she added. "You should go with me."

His immediate response surprised her. "Okay."

Her stomach bubbled and her legs tingled. "Okay, then. Should I call you when I get there?"

"I have a spare room," he offered. "You're welcome to it."

As much as she wanted full access to Greg, she understood it was best to have her own room. "It's fine. My mom is a travel agent, so she'll make the arrangements for me."

"That's cool. I have annual passes to just about anywhere you want to go, so just let me know where you want to meet tomorrow."

She glanced at the time. With luck, she'd be in Orlando at six o'clock the next morning.

"Noon sounds like a good time, and you're the local boy. Tell me the best place to go."

Greg chuckled. "I'm a movie nerd, so Hollywood Studios is my favorite place."

"If it has anything to do with a past galaxy a long time ago, then I know what you like most about it."

They shared a laugh, but neither one of them had much more to say. Every second she spoke to Greg made her feel almost dizzy.

"I guess I'm going to call my mom now, so she can get started with my reservations."

There was an awkward back and forth before they finally hung up. She was sad to end the call, but she was happy she had plans to meet him the next day.

She dialed her mother and placed the phone on her car's speaker. She figured she could get some driving done while they spoke.

"Azealia's Vacations," she answered.

"It's me, Mom. Don't you have caller ID?"

"I do, but I hardly look at it. What do you need?"

Azealia Turner always got to the point. She was busy with her hobbies and the life she'd created for herself when she left Paige and her father in Erwin, so she seldom had time to chat.

"I need you to book a hotel for me."

"Oh, that's entirely different, darling. I thought you were calling me to discuss some silliness."

"You mean, my life and what's going on it?" Paige responded flatly.

"Don't be ridiculous. I've grown tired of reading, so your profession is not interesting to me."

Paige wanted to hit her with a witty comeback about her job, but as she needed her mother to arrange accommodations for her, she deemed it unwise.

"Look, Mom. I need you to find me a hotel in Orlando that's close to—"

"Orlando, Florida?" Her mother seemed outraged at the prospect.

"Is there another Orlando?"

"Well, I can't say if there is or isn't, but why on earth would you want to go there?"

Paige's grip on the steering wheel tightened. "There's plenty of things to do there."

"If you're a child."

Paige took a deep breath. If she could get through their conversation, her mother would text and email her reservations and any other particulars.

"I'm meeting a man at Hollywood Studios tomorrow, and—"

"A date!" her mother practically squealed. "Why didn't you say so?"

Paige knew it was the best way to handle her mother. She valued independence, but her mother also believed women should date often.

"Can you get me tickets, too?"

"Let me look up the best place to stay, and I'll book it for you."

They said their goodbyes, complete with air kisses, and Paige's speaker went silent. She turned on the radio and landed on a great song.

Hours melted away as she sang and bounced in her seat to stay awake. She stopped to get gas and bought an apple. She'd read somewhere that an apple could give a person a boost of energy, similar to the effects of drinking caffeine, and it seemed to work. Either because it pumped up her body or because she chose to believe what she'd read, the apple seemed to keep her alert long enough to cross into Jacksonville.

She pulled over as lightning blasted through the sky. Her mother had emailed her reservations, and she typed the address to the resort into her GPS. The storm eased up enough to jump back onto the road, and within a couple of miles, Paige could see clear skies and breaking dawn.

She was amazed to find that a room was available at the resort when she checked in. Her mother had called ahead and pulled some strings with a reservation specialist.

The air was warm, even during the first week of December, and the air smelled like a swamp. Still, she breathed it in, happy to be surrounded by high-spirited vacationers.

Her room was on the ground level, and it had a view of the pool in the distance. The temple that acted as a slide was clearly identifiable. Even though her room wasn't decorated with cartoon characters, there was still a presence of Disney. Her television was on when she entered, and classic cartoons spilled from the speakers.

Her mother had found the best deal for tickets by adding a resort stay. The other tickets she'd secured were reasonable without buying a package, and Paige wasn't sure how she'd done it, but her mother had used her discount for one of them.

Paige slipped off her shoes and climbed into the bed farthest away from the door. She felt a chill in the room, but she was too tired to adjust the temperature.

She fell asleep thinking about Greg. She was excited about seeing him later that day, and her mind settled on the memory of the first time she met him a little over a year ago.

Chapter 15

Paige was extremely uncomfortable.

Everyone seemed to have a date. Even Daisey, who rarely had a man around her, held the arm of a well-dressed guy who was a little better than half her age. Petal was bouncing on her other side, excited to be part of her mother's special event.

Daisey had decided to throw a birthday party for herself. She was turning forty, and she had done so well in her investments that she'd made a lot of enemies.

Several of her cousins milled about the room, but the bulk of the crowd included the authors she'd published. It was a strange dynamic, as most writers were outgoing or reclusive. There was never really a balance, so one side of the room was filled with talkative partygoers who were laughing and dancing silly, and the other side had bodies who wished they had come up with a good excuse to be somewhere else. Paige was debating whether she should fake a headache or stomach cramps when he caught her eye.

He had finished speaking with another author, and he was refilling his punch glass. She thought about going over and saying something witty, but words escaped her. It was much easier in her novels. She could make her characters say anything, and she controlled the other characters' reactions, so it all worked out.

She concentrated on the music, hoping the soft sounds would help her acclimate to the atmosphere. She hummed along and sipped champagne.

"You're Paige Turner, aren't you?"

She stared at him fully, standing inches away from her. His hair was slicked back, and his brown eyes caught every fairy light in the room.

She opened her mouth to answer, and champagne spilled out. *How could she have forgotten to swallow it?*

He handed her a napkin from the table behind them, and she sopped up the liquid before it spread to her dress. She was certain that she was blushing, but the lighting was low enough to cover most of it.

"I didn't mean to startle you," he said.

He looked like he was trying to be sincere, but his mouth kept turning up at the corners. If she were honest, she couldn't blame him. She'd laugh at someone who'd ejected liquid down their chin.

"That's okay," she told him. "Usually, I remember to swallow anything in my mouth before I speak."

Her comment permitted him to let go of the laugh he'd been holding, and she found herself giggling.

"Are you with someone tonight?" He motioned to all the couples.

"No, I'm divorced."

"I know," he said, "but I thought you might be here with someone."

"No, I'm all yours."

As soon as she'd said it, she felt her knees grow weak from embarrassment. Bile inched up her throat, but she swallowed it down.

"I mean, I'm here alone."

"A beautiful woman should never be alone," he said and gave her a wink.

She couldn't continue their playful banter, so she turned their conversation into something more professional. She spoke about his debut novel and the success it had enjoyed.

Greg returned her compliments with accolades about her books and writing awards. He stayed close, but their bodies never brushed. Anyone who saw them would think they were colleagues sharing a pleasant conversation.

"Do you dance?" he asked.

"Only if my partner enjoys sore toes."

He smiled and looked out at the dance floor. "Give me a minute."

She watched him approach the DJ and toss some money into his jar. The music he selected boomed out of the speakers before he made his way back to her.

Paige pretended she was busy sorting through her clutch. She looked up when she caught his shoes in her peripheral vision.

He held out his arm. "I haven't had my toes stepped on in a while. Will you do me the honor?"

She accepted his arm, and he led her out onto the dance floor. They were in a comfortable position away from the limelight and close to the door.

Paige wrapped her arms around his neck as his hands linked behind her. They swayed easily.

"It's like a middle school dance," he said, nodding to the distance between them.

"Or like Catholic mixers where they tell the kids to leave enough space between them for the Holy Spirit."

She closed the space between them as much as she could without making their position awkward. One of her fingers ran down the back of his neck as she moved, and he shivered.

"I'm sorry."

"It's okay," he told her.

The song was slow but powerful, and most of the chatter in the room seemed to slow down as it played. Paige watched Greg's expression, curious why he'd selected the song. He sang some of the chorus, and as he did, he looked into her eyes. Paige tried to concentrate on the words to see if he was attempting to convey their meaning to her, but she was lost, swimming in a sea of emotions.

The song was over too soon, but another slow song started. Greg kept his arms around her, so Paige stayed in place.

"How many songs did you request?"

"Two," he admitted. "I didn't know if you'd like the first one."

"I did," she said. "I like all reasonable music."

His eyebrow arched. "What's 'reasonable music'?"

It was a simple question to answer, as she'd put her preference in her author bio, so people asked her about it frequently. "I'm not a fan of music that degrades any person."

"So, you even like the traditional tub thumpers?" he joked.

A squeal of delight interrupted them. With their slow movements, she and Greg had sashayed closer to Daisey, her date, and Petal. They had almost a front-row seat to the spectacle.

"Daddy!"

The young girl ran to her father with her blonde curls bouncing against her fluffy pink dress. Evan caught her, holding her to him and closing his eyes.

From the sweat on his face and the unkempt hair falling across his face, Paige could tell he had been drinking. She knew his breakup with Daisey had been hard, but she hadn't expected him to show up without an invitation.

"You weren't invited," Daisey said simply as he approached the table. Petal lay against her father's chest, drawing circles on his lapel.

"I thought it was an oversight." He flashed a smile at the people around Daisey's table, and they all laughed uncomfortably.

"I need you to leave now," Daisey said through clenched teeth. "You're ruining my party."

"How?" He rubbed noses with Petal. "As I see it, you invited all the authors of Daisey Flowers Publications, and you made sure to chain me to your company for a decade, so here I am."

"I don't want you here." Daisey picked the napkin off her lap and slung it onto her plate. Her date tried to keep her in her seat, but she rose and advanced on Evan.

Evan held Petal away as Daisy yelled at him. He stared beseechingly at the other people in the group, but no one offered to take the child away from the argument.

"How dare you show up here with a girl half your age and expect me to sit and smile?"

Evan looked behind him, and several feet away, a young blonde with pouty lips and a short black dress wandered around aimlessly. The men around her stared, as her heels were too high and her skirt was too short for Daisey to have invited her, especially since the publisher was lamenting the last minutes of her thirties.

Evan presented a lame defense. "She was supposed to wait in the car."

"It's an easy mistake," Daisey quipped. "She probably doesn't know what a car is."

Evan glanced at Daisey's date. "And I guess Mr. Beefcake over there is just a little better. He may have graduated high school this year."

Daisey's date appeared dazed by Evan's comment. "I'm twenty-nine." He looked from Evan to the people around him.

Petal had hidden her face, and her body shook with tears. Evan felt her little body trembling and held up his hand. "I'm sorry. I didn't know you were going to bring our daughter to—"

"*Our* daughter?" Daisey screeched. "Was she *our* daughter when I was staying home alone with her so you could visit your therapist?" She looked back at the people at her table. "He was banging her."

Paige had heard enough. She smiled apologetically at Greg and hurried over to Evan. Without a word, he understood she was there to help, and he encouraged Petal to go with her.

"So, you're on his side?" Daisey screamed at her.

With Petal's arms wrapped around her, Paige didn't engage in the argument. Evan wasn't the only one who had drunk too much alcohol, and once Daisey started yelling, she wouldn't stop until there was physical violence or someone dragged her away kicking and screaming.

"I guess you're sleeping with her, too," Daisey said to Evan when it was clear Paige wasn't taking the bait.

"I'm not sleeping with Paige," Evan defended. "I gave Petal to her so she didn't have to hear her mother rave on like a banshee. You act like I gave her to Cindy." He jerked his thumb at the girl behind him.

When she heard her name, Cindy rushed up to Evan, a huge smile on her uncomprehending face. "Did you need me, baby?"

Daisey laughed dryly. "Oh, this is Cindy." She shook her head. "Of course her name is Cindy."

Evan pointed at her. "Now, don't you go down *that* road. I told you who Cindy was."

Their voices faded out as Paige took Petal into another room. Once she put the child's feet on the hard tile of the cold, empty space, Paige squatted down, careful to keep the folds of her dress from revealing anything improper.

"Hey, Petal. I'm Paige. I'm going to take care of you until your mom and dad can figure things out."

The girl nodded, rubbing her eyes with the backs of her hands. "They fight a lot."

Paige tried to think of a way to change the subject, but Petal kept talking. "Daddy doesn't sleep at home anymore. Mommy made him go, and I hate her."

Paige's heart went out to Petal. She was dealing with her own feelings about the breakup between her mother and father, and their constant bickering confused her even more.

"Daddy came here to see *me*," she declared. "Mommy should let me go with him."

Paige didn't think Petal needed to be around either of her parents in their current conditions, but she bit her tongue. Sometimes, people just needed to vent, and she hoped she was helping Petal by letting her talk about her feelings.

"I hate her," she voiced again.

Paige stood up, and when Petal looked up at her, she said, "Hate is a strong emotion, but do you know what else is a stronger emotion?"

Petal continued to stare at her with Evan's eyes and Daisey's determined chin. Paige hoped she didn't sound basic to the young girl. She was intelligent for her age, but she was still a child, and Paige had one chance to gain her attention.

"Love. Love is a stronger emotion than hate."

Petal looked away. Paige hadn't said anything to warrant her attention.

Paige tried another angle. "I had to learn to love both my parents when they divorced."

Petal's expression turned inquisitive. "Your parents aren't together?"

Paige shook her head. "And when I got older, I was glad they didn't stay together. It was too hard for them."

Petal was considering her words when the door opened. Greg brought in a glass of punch and a bag of chips.

He introduced himself to Petal, handing her the refreshments. She took them, opening the cheesy bag of chips with her teeth.

The door opened again, and Daisey's frazzled assistant breezed into the room. She hadn't been a party guest, so she had dressed in jeans and a tee shirt.

"Daisey wants Petal to go home with me," she told Paige and Greg.

"Sierra!" Petal cried out happily.

Seeing the situation with the child was resolved, Greg led Paige out the back door of the room. The night air was turning crisp, but it didn't have a strong bite.

He took off his suit jacket and placed it around her shoulders. A smile tickled Paige's lips as she accepted the gesture of her handsome companion.

It wasn't the first time she had noticed his long nose and perfectly trimmed beard. She hoped the champagne wouldn't make her too giddy about his appearance and affect her ability to talk to him.

They walked the length of the building and stared up at the sky. The sky was full of stars, and they sparkled with possibilities.

Paige longed for him to touch her. Just one hand on her arm would make it easier for her to fall back into their playful banter.

"It was a long drive," he said, yawning.

Paige's spirits fell. *Was that a hint that he wanted to go to his hotel?*

"You drove?"

He pointed to his blue truck in the parking lot. "It wasn't bad except in Georgia. They have police posted everywhere."

"Did you drive all the way up here for Daisey's party?"

He laughed and put his hands in his pockets. "Not exactly. Daisey made it clear she expected all her authors to be here, but I scheduled a book signing in Knoxville to offset a little of the money I lost by coming up here."

"You lost money?"

He pointed at a shooting star, but instead of using the moment to embrace the romance, he carried on with their general conversation. "Yeah, I work in construction."

Before Paige knew what she was doing, she reached out and touched his bicep, squeezing it. She dropped her hand when Greg stared at it.

She slipped out of his jacket and handed it to him. "That's probably enough fun for me for one night."

Instead of taking his jacket, he pulled Paige into him. She had seconds to breathe in his fresh, woodsy scent before he lowered his mouth to meet her lips.

She'd never thought a kiss tasted sweet until that moment. Their tongues moved in synch, as if powered by the stars or the gentle wind in the trees. Like the start of a light buzz, Paige's mind floated around them and everything else faded away.

He broke their contact, breathing heavily. Paige was glad she'd had the same effect on him. She moistened her lips and tasted the kiss he'd left behind.

"Stop touching me!" a voice boomed as the door next to them swung open.

Daisy staggered in her heels as her date followed behind her. He carried her purse and jacket and tried to steady her as she tried unsuccessfully to step into the parking lot.

"I told you to keep your hands off me," Daisey said to him.

He held his hands up. "I need to get you home. You're—"

She rounded on him, her finger swaying like branches in the wind. "I'm not leaving with you. You took his side."

"I didn't side with Evan," he defended. "I just said you should let him see his daughter. You know, when he's not drunk."

"And let his floozies around her?" She let out a bitter laugh. "No, thanks."

"Do you want me to drive you home?" Paige offered.

Daisey narrowed her eyes at her date. "No, I want him to take me home." She pointed to Greg.

Greg was shocked, but he accepted the coat and purse when Daisey's date handed them over. Even though she'd discarded him, the man made sure Daisey was secure in Greg's truck before he got into his own vehicle.

Paige realized she still had Greg's jacket as he was driving away. She texted him about it, but he didn't respond until much later.

Evan filtered out with his date as Paige left. He burst through the doors as if he were triumphant.

"Paige," he called out to her. "Come here."

Paige didn't move, but he joined her, throwing his arm around her shoulder. The pressure caused her to bend a little to meet his height.

His bubbly companion sidled up next to him. "Is she going to go back with us?"

Evan considered it. "Why don't you come to my room and have some fun?" His eyes darted as he spoke, and liquor fumed off him.

Paige shook her head. "I have to get home."

"No one's waiting for you there," he said.

His statement shocked her. She had been vocal about her recent divorce, and she hadn't brought a date with her, but it was rude of him to point out her obvious loneliness.

Adopting a carefree attitude, Paige stepped into the parking lot. "I don't need the drama right now. I'll be content at home by myself."

A smile inched across his lips. Evan wasn't used to rejection, and it didn't suit him.

"It looked like you would have been content with Greg tonight. But he went home with Daisey." He stared off in the direction they had driven. "Tough luck, kid. You know she's almost as ruthless with men as I am with women."

Evan's date giggled as if his slight didn't apply to her. Paige felt sorry for the girl.

"Like I said, Evan, I don't need the drama right now." And then, because she couldn't resist making a jab of her own, she added, "Petal is fine, by the way. I may not be a parent, but I don't think a child should see her parents arguing and inebriated."

As she'd hoped, the smile slipped off his face. She turned on her heels and walked to her car. Once she assessed that all the effects of the alcohol she'd consumed were gone, she drove home.

For once, she had limited her alcohol intake, and she could remember every part of the evening perfectly. If it hadn't been for Greg, she would have needed to call a driver, as she would have drunk as much of Daisey's expensive champagne as possible.

When she went to sleep, she thought of Greg, tasting her lips to see if any vestiges of his kiss remained. When she woke, she inhaled deeply and smiled, thinking of his arms wrapped around her.

She toasted pastries and brought them to the table, scrolling down her social media feed. Daisy's name caught her eye, and she wondered if the woman had posted about her intense hangover.

Paige lost her appetite as her eyes landed on a picture of Greg lying across a bed. His suit was on, but the bedclothes beneath him were crumpled. Anyone else would have only seen a tall, dark-haired man, but Paige recognized his profile instantly. He had spent the night in Daisey's bed.

Almost immediately, her phone lit up with a message. When she saw it was from Greg, she avoided reading it for hours, narrowing her eyes at her phone when it came into view.

She read his message in the early afternoon. He had asked if she'd like to bring some of her books and go to the book signing with him. If she hadn't seen the post, she would have jumped at the chance to be with him again. Paige returned his text, claiming that she'd just seen the message. She explained it was for the best, as she had a busy day ahead of her.

They exchanged pleasantries but made no other plans. Months later, Paige couldn't shake the memory of her time with Greg, but she tried to give professional platitudes without a hint of romantic interest. Finally, they settled into a friendly routine of mutual support for their work.

Paige had avoided a possible triangle with her publisher, and she was glad to leave it alone. But as the months fell from the calendar, she couldn't help but wonder what would have happened that night if she and Greg would have shared just a few more moments under a sky full of stars.

Chapter 16

Greg was already waiting for her at the entrance to the park. Her mother had linked her ticket to a band on her wrist, so she went through a line while Greg waited for his pass to be verified.

Once inside, the park opened before her. There was so much to do, and Greg pulled her along, as he insisted the best rides were at the back of the park.

Spaceships and aliens confirmed her suspicions about her date. "You're a George Lucas fan."

He only smiled in response and pointed to a ride. They spent three hours in the representation of a historical galaxy far away, and by noon, they had ridden two rides and visited a bar with strange milk.

"Those really must be the most popular rides in the park," Paige commented.

"This is a pretty popular park," he replied. "Most people like to come here."

They sampled some food from stands set up by separate vendors. The doughnuts and pretzels were sweet and salty delights, and Paige loved the pineapple float she used to wash them down.

They waited in lines for an extended period of time, and it gave Paige and Greg time to talk. Even in December, the sun was hot, but she found little ways to get close to him, like when they moved forward in line or let people pass whose family members had saved a place in line for them.

"Is it hot to you?" she asked him.

He looked down at her. "No. In Florida, it's hot in July and August. Seventy-five degrees is sweater weather."

She rolled her eyes at his joke. As the temperatures were much colder in Tennessee, she hadn't brought shorts, so she'd bought a short-sleeved shirt from the shop at her resort and donned a pair of black leggings. The dark material made her legs sweat in the afternoon sun, and her legs had never perspired.

They settled into a closed compartment to experience a free fall, and as everyone else was shaking with fear from the ghostly sounds and visions, Paige trembled as Greg put his fingers into her hand. She gripped the handrail with her other hand and tried to keep from squeezing his hand too tightly as the attraction lifted and dropped them.

The park closed with a brilliant show. The area was almost full, but Greg found a good place for them and stood behind her, with his arms draped over her shoulders, as the show played before them.

Just as the presentation reached its climax, Greg turned her to face him. Lifting her chin gently, he placed a kiss on her lips. It didn't last long, but it reminded her of their time at Daisey's birthday party.

He walked her to the bus that was waiting to take her to her resort. She didn't want their day to end, but she wasn't sure about the right way to continue their date without encouraging him to think she wanted something more physical.

"Do you want to go with me?" she asked. "Just for a little while," she amended. "The pool is open until eleven, and we could have a drink at the resort's bar."

He shook his head. "I have...something I need to do."

She quickly evaluated his response. *Did he want to go with her, but he had other obligations, or was he rejecting her for another reason?*

He bent to kiss her before she left, but she pretended not to notice his effort. She ducked away and waved at him from the bus.

"Where can I meet you tomorrow?" he spoke over the bus's motor.

"At the castle," she called back.

She had mixed feelings about her date with Greg. On one hand, he was funny, kind, and personable, but there always seemed to be something holding him back. *Did he think of Daisey when he was with Paige, and did he long for the night he'd shared with their publisher?*

Or was it much worse? Paige's mind raced as she panicked. *Was he married?*

She tried to console herself as she remembered his author bio and none of his interviews mentioned a spouse. Besides, she doubted a significant other would let him spend two full days in a row with her.

Greg seemed to like her. Every time they'd been together, outside of the interview in Johnson City, he had kissed her. *Was he holding back because they lived in separate places?*

She was glad he had spent time with her, but she knew it was coming to a close. He worked, and there were only so many days he could take off. She concluded she would put her concerns to the side and enjoy the time they had together.

At her resort, she felt lonely for the first time. Happy families were grabbing a late-night meal before heading to bed, and couples soaked up the atmosphere before returning to their love nests for the night. She sat on the edge of her bed, listening to the wet slaps feet made against the concrete as children raced from the pool to catch up with their parents.

She was ready for a relationship. If Greg had returned to the resort with her, she wouldn't have let him go. She had never been a fan of long-distance relationships, but she would have tried one with him.

Sure, he had slept with their publisher after he'd kissed Paige, but Daisey was alluring, and they said nothing about a romantic entanglement. Obviously, the night meant nothing to Daisey and Greg, as they acted like professionals, and they stayed away from each other when Greg had been in town for the interview.

Paige showered, and as the water ran over her, she felt a spark of inspiration. She wasn't going to wait for Greg to ask her about dating. She was going to ask him, and nothing was going to stand in her way.

Chapter 17

Paige worried when he was almost fifteen minutes late. Even though Greg had texted her he'd had to deal with something, she was still nervous. *Was the "something" another lover?*

She sat on a brick wall, hearing carnival music with hints of songs from popular movies in her head, as she kicked her feet. Paige looked for a single man in the crowds that approached the entrance, but the glare from the small lake in front of her and the rising morning sun made it difficult to see. She finally settled on watching the breeze off the water blow a map of the park down the sidewalk. It stopped at her feet as if it considered resting there, but the wind picked it up and carried it further away.

"Hey."

Greg's breathless voice got her attention. She stood up, ready to share more time with him, but then she saw the reason for his lateness.

A boy stood at his side. He was a mirror of his father and was no more than eight years old. The only difference in their features was the boy's hair-free face and snaggle-toothed grin.

Greg noticed her stare and brought the boy forward. "Paige, this is Alan. He's the reason I'm late."

The boy stared up at his dad. "We could've been on time if you'd left when I told you to."

While they had their exchange, Paige went through everything she thought she'd known about Greg. He had never mentioned a child. Family was something Daisey brought to the surface, but for some reason, she'd kept Alan's existence out of the limelight.

Paige let them guide her into the park. The sudden appearance of Greg's son shocked her, but she continued to smile and nod at all the appropriate intervals, so he wouldn't realize the depth of her surprise.

Greg bought the boy a balloon, and while he was paying for it, Alan spoke to her. "Grammy's sick. She couldn't watch me today."

At first, his voice startled Paige. She had no recollection of when she'd begun conversing with adults, but she'd assumed it was at an early age, as there was no one in her father's house in the woods to play with. Their conversation was commonplace to Alan, so she tried to treat it that way.

"Well, you get to enjoy a day at the park, so it's not a terrible thing."

"She's throwing up everywhere,'" he added with emphasis.

Paige rushed to explain. "I was talking about the way the day turned out for you. Your Grammy's sickness is terrible. I hope she feels better soon."

"Me, too," he said, "because Dad said I had to go back to school tomorrow, and Grammy picks me up."

They rode rides all morning, and Paige was mostly silent. It didn't seem out of place, as they were boarding, riding, and disembarking. She was only truly uncomfortable at lunch when Greg left her at a table with Alan while he ordered their meals from the employee at a nearby food stand.

"Do you do drugs?"

Paige was taken off guard by the young child's question. She wondered what had prompted him to ask it. *Had she swayed too heavily or seemed dizzy after the rides?*

"No, I've never taken drugs."

The boy seemed skeptical. "Not even when the doctor prescribed them?"

Paige amended her statement. "Yes. I have taken antibiotics when I was sick."

"Oh, that's how my mom got addicted to drugs. The doctor prescribed them to her and—"

Paige couldn't help but interrupt. "She got addicted to antibiotics? They're non-narcotic."

The last word seemed to give Alan some trouble as he sought to digest it. Paige tried to help him out.

"Antibiotics are what the doctor gives you when you're sick. Narcotics can be given when a person's in an immense amount of pain."

He pointed at her. "That's it. My mom was hurting all the time after her car wreck, and—"

Greg joined them, placing fries and pretzels on the table. His smile dropped when he noticed the abrupt silence.

"What did I miss?"

Alan looked at Paige, and she understood they had been discussing a taboo topic. "You know, just getting-to-know-you stuff." It wasn't untrue, but the lie sat sourly in her stomach.

Alan seemed grateful, and he stuffed the soft pretzel into his mouth after he deconstructed it. The fries remained untouched until Greg gave his son what remained of his pretzel and ate them.

Paige forced herself through her fries and gave Alan her pretzel. It amazed her that he still had room in his stomach for it, but the small boy polished it off as they headed into a haunted ride.

The atmosphere was spooky, but Alan took it in stride. "I was scared of this ride when I was three," he informed her. "But I'm seven now, and I know the ghosts aren't real."

Paige hadn't attempted to flirt with Greg that day, and Alan had sat between them for most of the rides, but the fast-moving vestibule kept them from choosing their seats, and Paige was sandwiched between Alan and Greg.

In the darkest part of the ride, while a woman spoke through a crystal ball, Greg attempted to kiss her. He tried to move her face with his fingers on her chin, but she jerked away. She wasn't comfortable showing affection around Alan.

In the late afternoon, Alan rubbed his eyes and whined about the number of steps they had to take between rides. When soothing his son with a water ride didn't work, Greg told her he had to go.

She gave the boys a friendly wave. Greg kept looking at her over his shoulder, and he mouthed something to her, but she couldn't read lips, so she dismissed it.

As much as she had enjoyed their company, Paige was content with running around the park by herself. She chose her rides based on her mood and the number of people in line, and she casually browsed through the shops, buying a magnet for herself and one for her mother as a gesture of appreciation for setting up the vacation for her.

Her phone vibrated in her pocket, but she ignored it. The fresh pops of fireworks sounded overhead, and she gathered with a mass of people in front of the castle to view them.

A family in front of her reminded Paige of the people she knew from her hometown. The children had dressed in nice clothes, but the clothes frayed at the seams with age, indicating that they'd gone through more than one child. The parents seemed happy, but there was a disconnection between them. Even though they held onto each other, it seemed forced, like they were on a lifeboat sailing across raging emotions.

The mother noticed Paige's stare, and she handed her a camera. Without a word, Paige spent the next five minutes snapping photographs of the family with the fireworks as the backdrop. When she finished, she handed the camera back to the woman.

She wondered how long the couple had been married. *Had their obvious financial situation caused the distance between the woman and her husband, or was it the children?*

She'd always believed her dad had a long list of women because he only used them to fulfill his needs. He spent the rest of his time raising her. *Was that what she was to Greg? Did he want to sleep with her and keep his bachelor lifestyle while he raised his son?*

There must have been other women Greg had seen during his years as a single father. Paige remembered her father and the women he'd tried to keep from her. Her father had dedicated his life to raising Paige, but there were nights that he left her with a babysitter and returned just before sunrise.

Her father never talked to her about the women until she was a teen and confronted him about them. Even then, he kept her separate from them. It was only after she entered college and stayed in her dorm that she started running into the women when she'd visit. She never saw them more than once, though, so she'd flush their names as soon as she'd heard them.

Greg had introduced her to his son, though. *Did that mean something, or was it only because of caretaking issues?*

She could dwell on the *what-ifs* and *whys* all night, but she put them out of her mind. She was so exhausted that she hardly got through a shower and dropped onto her bed without drying her hair.

She didn't see Greg's message until the next morning when she was on her way to Sea World. He had asked her about her emotional distance and told her he had to work, so he'd miss her next park.

She sent back a light-hearted message, telling him how much she had enjoyed her time with Alan and him, and wishing him a safe day at work. She tried to put it out of her mind, but it wasn't as fun viewing the animals and riding the rides without him. In a way, she even missed Alan's random conversations and wondered if he would rather be with her than at school.

After lunch, she felt her phone vibrating in her pocket. She saw it was Greg, and debated ignoring it, before deciding to take the call.

He got right to the point. "Can you pick up Alan at school?"

"What?"

"My mom has been sick," he went on. "We thought it was a virus, but it was her gallbladder. I'm with her now, and they're prepping her for emergency surgery."

Paige wanted to give him a response, but it was such a shift from her laid-back mood to chaos that she was at a loss for words. Her mouth found them, though, and pushed out an answer before her brain caught up.

"Sure."

There was an audible sigh of relief from the other end of the line. He gave her the directions and told her he'd call her when he left the hospital.

Thankfully, the school had received a message with her name and the description of her car, so once the teacher in the pickup line saw her driver's license, she released Alan's hand and he climbed into the backseat. He buckled the belt and looked at her expectantly in the rearview mirror.

"I don't have a car seat," she said apologetically. "Is it against the law to drive without one?"

He shrugged his shoulders. "Daddy has one for me, but the doctor said I was tall for my age."

Paige wasn't certain what he meant, so she resolved to have him in her car for as little time as possible. Unfortunately, Greg hadn't told her where to take Alan once she picked him up, and the boy didn't have a key to his house, so Paige was at a loss.

"I could go to your house," Alan suggested.

"My house is in Tennessee, sweetie, and I doubt your dad wants me to take you there."

His idea sparked a decision, and Paige drove back to Sea World. As she stood at the gate paying for Alan's ticket, he asked, "Do you get snow in Tennessee?"

His innocent question made her smile. "We get a fair share of snow in the winter."

He kicked a tab from a can. "I wish I could see the snow."

"You'll have to come up sometime," she told him. She realized how much her statement meant to him when she looked down at his wide eyes.

"Really? Do you have a sled, too?"

She thought of her mother's old wooden sled. It probably wasn't safe, but she could grab one from a discount store pretty easily. "I think I could find one."

He stopped at the first animal attraction, and they spent a fair share of time watching penguins. It shocked Paige when he held her hand throughout the park.

They had a quiet dinner, and after he ate, Alan blinked his eyes. Paige recognized the signs and led them to the exit.

At her resort, Paige turned down the other bed for Alan and waited for Greg's call. She drifted to sleep, wondering if her feelings about children were changing.

Chapter 18

It seemed later than ten o'clock at night when her phone rang. All the walking she'd done had made her muscles tired, and they felt glazed with exhaustion as she searched for her vibrating phone.

Greg's mother's surgery had gone well, but it had taken longer, and he didn't explain the reason. He told Paige he was on his way to her resort, and he knocked on her door within forty-five minutes.

He saw Alan asleep on the bed, fully fed, showered, and dressed in clothes from the resort's gift shop. "Thank you for this. I usually rely on my mom or brother, but—" He held up his hands.

He looked exhausted. Paige ordered room service and directed him to the shower. He had a small bag with him, and he told her he always carried it in his truck in case of emergencies.

After his shower, he picked at the meal she'd collected from the cafeteria. "I can drive back home," he insisted, but after Paige saw several expressive yawns, she told him to stay.

He looked at the bed, and Alan had his back turned to them. Greg took Paige in his arms and kissed her deeply. She felt herself melting into him.

"I wish I'd have gotten a two-bedroom suite," she said between kisses.

"I'll pay for one right now if they have it," he joked.

Their touches grew more intense until they were wrapped together on Paige's bed. She wanted him to slip between her sheets and continue, but Alan spoke in his sleep.

They jerked away from each other, worried about him rolling over and seeing them in an intimate embrace. Greg ran a hand through his hair.

"I want to be with you, but—"

Paige interrupted him. "You don't have to explain. It would be too weird to sneak into the bathroom while Alan was asleep in the next room."

He didn't get close to her or try to kiss her again. After a few minutes, he laid down with Alan, facing her. They closed their eyes at the same time, and it seemed like she blinked, and it was morning.

After he rushed through getting Alan ready for school, Greg promised Paige he'd come back to the resort after he checked on his mother. Alan hugged her, and she watched them walk away through the large picture window in her room.

She welcomed the silence after they were gone. She showered and thought about breakfast, but the bed was so inviting she climbed back into it.

A gentle tapping woke her. She opened the door, and Greg followed her to the bed.

At first, she thought they were only going to sleep, but after he started kissing her neck, they didn't stop until hours later. She pulled the sheets off the floor that they'd kicked off in their frenzied desire to be with each other.

"Don't you need to pick up Alan soon?"

"I have a friend picking him up," he replied. "She'll keep him as long as I need her to."

Paige wondered about the friend Greg had mentioned. *Was she the wife of one of his close buddies, or was she a past lover?*

She thought about asking him, but she put the thoughts away. There was no reason to start their relationship with jealousy. It had ruined her marriage.

"I'll need to go sit with my mom soon, but do you want to have" — he glanced at his phone, and his eyes widened at the time — "a late lunch?"

She giggled. "Sure. Let me shower and get ready."

She hurried, but when she emerged, he'd left a note telling her he was waiting for her in the lobby. They ordered some sandwiches and fruit and ate with a view of the pool.

"I can't tell you how relieved I am that my mom is okay," he told her. "We were really worried because she never—"

A worker dropped a tray behind her, and Paige jumped. She felt her heart pick up speed and her face flush, and before she knew it, she was running.

Time she couldn't remember darkened her vision. When she understood her surroundings again, she was in her car, and Greg was beating on the door. She fumbled for the switch that controlled the window, and when it wouldn't work, she opened the door.

"What happened?" he demanded. "Why did you run off?"

Paige didn't want to talk to him about the abuse she'd endured or the therapy she'd had to try to get over it. Two resort employees were standing at a distance, though, and she needed to let them know the basics about her situation.

Paige took a deep breath and stepped out of her car. Greg caught her when her shaky legs wouldn't support her.

Paige stared at the workers until they approached her. She waved away their concerns.

"I'm fine," she told them. "I have PTSD. I'm sorry I reacted so strangely." She kept herself from looking at Greg or measuring his reaction to her admission.

"You were in the military," one of them said.

It wasn't a question, but Paige treated it like one. She could have let them think her display had to do with a difficult tour of duty, but it would have been disrespectful to the other men and women who had served her country.

"No," she responded. "I have it for a different reason."

She was certain there was an employee protocol, and when the workers assessed she was safe and wasn't a threat to anyone else, they backed away. She could see them talking to each other as they stepped into the lobby, and she knew they were discussing the situation.

Greg walked her to her room. Once she was lying on her bed, he asked, "Can you tell me what happened?"

"I had an episode of post-traumatic stress," she told him. "I was in a bad relationship, and sometimes loud sounds will cause me to go into a fight-or-fly response."

Greg smoothed her hair back. Paige wasn't thrilled with the gesture, but she allowed it. She wanted to be someone he longed for and couldn't stop thinking about, but she was turning into a burden. She could feel the change, and she hated it.

"What happened, Paige? What did he do that caused this?"

Greg may have been sincere, but Paige was too worried about the shift from the flirty and fun part of their relationship to the serious turn it had taken. "I'm really fine. It was nothing."

He held her and tried to talk to her again, but she kept her distance. An embrace she would have melted into before the incident felt forced and void of emotion. She distanced herself from his attempts, only providing him with faux smiles and light-hearted answers.

Finally, Greg had to leave. "They'll be expecting me at the hospital. Can Alan and I stop by tonight?"

"Sure," she said, smiling, and accepting the kiss he placed on her lips.

She tried to savor that last moment of affection, as she had no intention of being there when he came back.

Chapter 19

Always leave them wanting more.

Her mother had said that to Paige every time she prepared to leave her boyfriends. She'd even said it as she left Paige and her father, expelling it as a piece of advice as Paige watched her walk to her red convertible from the front steps of her dad's home.

After her episode, she couldn't imagine that Greg would want anything more to do with her. Instead of leaving him wanting more, she was going before he could politely end their blossoming relationship. It would hurt worse to see him silently waiting until Alan fell asleep so that he could tell her he wasn't interested in a relationship.

It took an hour to pack up and release her room. Guest services were very helpful, but she didn't accept their offer to carry her bags to her car.

Once she was on the road, she felt better. If she had to deal with her problems, she could do it at home. She'd had a nice little escape, but it was time to go back home.

She wasn't worried about her decision until she was two hours into her drive. Greg was a single father, and he was going to waste gas money to make a round trip to see her at her resort. And Alan had hugged her. She didn't want him to be disappointed, even though she'd never see him again.

She pulled over and typed out a quick text. She told Greg that she'd had an emergency, and she needed to go home. It was half-true. After all, her attack had been unexpected, and she didn't need to risk another one.

He responded almost immediately. She read the message twice, trying to push down the hope that bubbled in her chest.

He wasn't angry. He even asked to visit her after Christmas.

Later, as she lay on her couch, Paige filled her thoughts with Greg. Her therapist had warned her that most relationships weren't ready to deal with trauma until they were out of the beginning stages, but Greg seemed to handle it well.

She wanted to believe he was perfect for her, and that he could help put all her broken pieces back together, but it was a tall order for a new relationship. He'd wanted her to talk about what led to her trauma, but she wasn't sure she'd ever be able to tell him any more about Nathan or the last night she saw her ex-husband.

***

Paige often dreamed of Nathan, and it was never good. She woke up in cold sweats with the feeling her screams had pulled her from her nightmares.

This time, he had seated her at the kitchen table as he berated her for burned food. She'd thought the steak was medium-well, but he told her she had blackened it.

She cut a piece to explain her point. "There's a little pink in the middle."

He picked up his steak. "You eat it then." It slumped in his hand before he threw it at her.

Paige tried not to react. She picked it up and placed it on her plate.

"Are you trying to get smart with me?" he asked, grabbing the collar of her shirt.

The action was so swift that it took her off guard. She tried not to panic, aware that he could sense the fear in her trembling form. Facing his tormented brown eyes was hard for Paige, and she didn't know what to say. She fumbled for anything that sounded like a right answer, but she wasn't fast enough.

Nathan threw her backward in her chair, and her head rattled against the linoleum floor. The pain was sharp and intense, but she hardly had time to register it before he pounced on her with a steak in his hand.

"Eat it," he commanded.

Paige wanted to be anywhere else, but she knew she had to do whatever he said. After he had shoved the steak halfway into her mouth, his rage simmered to anger.

He grabbed her stomach, bunching the skin until it pinched. He pressed on her belly until her eyes bulged.

"You don't like it, do you?" he jeered. "That's how I'll feel 'cause you don't know how to cook a steak."

Giving one more excruciating push, he lifted off her stomach. Paige gasped for air and threw up the steak he'd made her eat.

He pushed his arms into his jacket. Motioning to the vomit, he said, "It's probably for the best. You were getting a little on the heavy side."

She jolted into action when he slammed the door. Nathan could be gone for ten minutes or the rest of the night, but he'd beat her unmercifully if he found the apartment in a mess when he returned.

After she'd cleaned the mess, she pulled her laptop out of an almost hidden drawer in her entertainment center. She'd sent the manuscripts from the first four books in a series to a new publisher in the area, and she hoped the woman would like her characters.

When she checked her email, she was shocked to find an acceptance letter. The woman had suggested a meeting, but Nathan wasn't working, so she changed it to the time when he visited the Suboxone clinic each week. It was the one time she could count on his absence, as he wouldn't miss out on the refills of his buprenorphine and nerve pills. She hoped it would be an acceptable change.

She put her laptop away and sat on the couch, numbly staring at the television. She couldn't stand the noise anymore, preferring silence to the blaring voices.

She remembered too late that she hadn't brushed her teeth when the door opened. Nathan came in, with apologies and false promises. Everything was fine until he kissed her.

At first, she pulled away, but then he grabbed her chin and forced her mouth onto his. As soon as he tasted the vomit on her tongue, he retched.

She moved away, apologizing, and explaining that she'd forgotten to brush her teeth. She was almost out of range when he slapped her.

The sting of it brought tears to her eyes. He pounced on her, grabbing the skin on her sides, and squeezing it until Paige let out a cry. When she did, he head-butted her in the mouth.

"You won't forget to brush your teeth if you don't have any," he mocked.

Paige jerked awake and fought her sweaty blanket until she landed on the floor. She moved against the back of the couch and held her mouth. It throbbed from the blow it took in her dream, but the blood had dried years ago. Thankfully, she'd only received a busted lip and a few bruises from that experience, but the emotional scars ran much deeper.

She didn't know when she started crying, but once she felt the tears, she dried them. "He can't hurt me anymore," she said boldly as she climbed back into bed.

But she knew it wasn't true. Nathan was always in her thoughts, questioning her actions and degrading her. And according to his prison sentence, he'd be out of jail by Christmas, and who knew what he'd be capable of then.

Chapter 20

"What's going on?" Evan asked as his eyes darted on the screen, presumably looking from Paige to Greg. "Something's different."

Paige answered before Greg, not giving him a chance to minimize their relationship. "Nothing. Nothing has changed."

Greg's smile may have faltered for a moment, but she tried not to notice it. He repeated what she'd said with extra emphasis.

"You two slept together," Evan said, pointing at the screen. "Don't try to deny it. I can tell."

Paige opened her mouth to do just that, but she closed it with a pop. Greg smiled, and even though it was meant for her, Evan latched onto it.

"You sly dog! How was it?"

Paige couldn't remember seeing Greg embarrassed, but he colored. "W-Why don't you ask her?"

Evan wasn't deterred. "Fine. Paige, did Greg rock your world, or is there a need he didn't satisfy that I can help you with?"

Paige's mouth worked, but no sound came out.

"I see." Evan stroked his chin. "Well, it was either really good or really bad, so why don't you two quit making goofy faces at each other, and we'll get to work."

The rest of the meeting was productive and fun, and Paige learned she could separate the feelings she had for Greg as they exchanged constructive criticism about their work. He threw her a few quick winks during their discussion, mostly when Evan was looking in a different direction, but he maintained a professional demeanor.

"I'm not going to talk about the next scene tonight," Evan told them. "It may be too much for sensitive ears."

Paige rolled her eyes. "I've read all your books, Evan. Nothing you can say will surprise me."

Evan chuckled and launched into explicit detail about a sex scene between Cindy and a character Greg had created. Greg nodded along, agreeing with Evan's depiction of his character's actions.

Paige willed herself not to blush as Evan described things she'd never considered. *Did Greg want her to try the positions Evan had mentioned, and since Evan had mentioned them, was Greg thinking about trying them with her?*

She could feel her pulse in her face, so she tried to think of anything to keep her from turning a brighter red. She settled on organizing her underwear drawer in her head.

"What was that?" Greg asked.

Paige hoped she hadn't spoken aloud. She was in the middle of going through her cotton panties in her mind, so if she'd muttered something—

"Is someone there?" Evan asked. Both men looked alarmed.

Paige had been so caught up in her thoughts that she hadn't heard the noises. If her brain had registered them, it had dismissed them as sounds from Greg or Evan's houses.

When she focused, she could hear a man's voice yelling at someone to hurry. A crash of tinkling glass followed, and Paige fell to the floor.

***

She woke up in the hospital with a splitting headache.

The doctor who came into her room explained that it wasn't a migraine, and they were keeping her overnight to watch the concussion she had suffered. Paige's father held her hand as the doctor spoke, and Trish crossed her arms over her chest, a grave expression on her usually cheerful features.

"You were hit by a rock," her father told her when the doctor left.

"It was the size of a boulder," Trish said, but she looked away when Paige's father shot her a look.

Every word Paige spoke took an immense amount of concentration. "How did I get here?"

Her father looked at his companion and turned back to Paige. "Evan Donaldson called the police department. Lewis found you and called the ambulance."

It was strange, but the first thing she wondered was why Greg hadn't called the emergency services. *Was she less important to him than she'd thought?*

"Lewis had the rock with him," her father went on. "It was pretty sizable, but I don't see how it went through the window and hit you so hard."

"I was right in front of the window." Paige tried to turn to demonstrate her position, but every movement sent sharp pains through her head. "My back was to the glass."

Her father's mouth trembled, and he stood, dropping Paige's hand. "How could this happen? That son of a—"

"Jim," Trish cautioned. "Paige's head hurts, and you're getting loud."

He placed a hand on his forehead. "I'm sorry, princess. I just don't understand how this is happening while your ex-husband is still in jail."

"He's out," Trish announced.

All the blood seemed to drain out of Paige's body. The monster who had beaten her unmercifully was walking the streets again, and it seemed he was determined to keep hurting her.

***

"They let him go early?"

Trish nodded carefully. "He got out last week, and Sheriff Murphy railed them for not alerting you about it."

Paige thought about the unopened mail in her foyer. "I may have gotten a notice, but I didn't open it."

"What!" her father shouted. "You didn't open the letter?"

"I thought it had something to do with Nathan, so I avoided it. I couldn't deal with anything else after Willie James—"

"What about Willie James?" her father demanded.

Paige's head was throbbing, but she told him about the incident. "And I took the letter to Sheriff Murphy."

"But you didn't tell me about it?"

Paige closed her eyes, feeling as though her brain was swelling against her skull. "I left for Florida soon after that."

"Something else you didn't tell me about," he said. "I had to hear about it from your mom."

Paige sighed heavily. "I needed to get away fast, and mom secured my reservations. I never thought—"

"That's the problem," her father interrupted. "You don't think."

His remark chastised her, and Paige moved her eyes to the machines that kept time with her heartbeat. When she looked back at him, her father spoke kindly to her.

"I love you, princess, and your safety means the world to me." He looked up at Trish for confirmation before he spoke to Paige again. "I want you to stay with me again for a while."

Paige enjoyed having her own space. It did wonders for her creativity, but the nights were hard on her. She couldn't even sleep in her bedroom without feeling trapped.

"Okay."

Her father nodded, and Trish took a cleansing breath. She offered to get coffee, and Paige and her father didn't speak in Trish's absence.

Paige decided to sell her small home and search for another one. *But where could she go that Nathan wouldn't find her?*

Chapter 21

A soft touch on her hand woke her.

She stirred, and thinking it was her father, she asked, "Will you close the blinds?"

The light dimmed, and the touch returned. The fingers were more insistent, moving into her palm and causing her to open her eyes.

"Hey," Greg said.

Paige sat up quickly, the pain in her head reminding her she couldn't move fast. "What're you doing here?"

"After I told Evan to call 9-1-1, I grabbed Alan, and jumped into the truck." He glanced over at his son, who was sleeping peacefully on the visitor couch.

Paige was suddenly aware of how she looked and smelled. She hadn't checked her appearance since the accident, and the blood caked to her scalp hadn't been washed out of her hair.

Greg seemed to understand her awkwardness. "I'll go get a cup of coffee. I'll be back soon." He placed a kiss on her forehead and left.

She got up gingerly and brushed her teeth with the hospital kit in the bathroom. Other than washing her face and applying some lip balm, she could do nothing more until she took a shower.

She was a little dizzy on her way back to bed. Something that should have taken five minutes the previous day had taken almost fifteen minutes.

Greg came back with two cups. She was about to tell him she didn't drink coffee when she noticed the liquid inside her cup was much lighter.

"It's hot apple cider," Greg said. "I remembered you didn't like coffee, but I thought you might enjoy something warm to drink."

Even when he hadn't liked or commented on all her posts, he'd still read them. She'd written something about the evils of sweet tea and coffee, and he hadn't seemed to notice the post, but he must have read it.

She smiled. "Thank you."

Her eyes widened when she looked at Alan. He was still in a winter coat, buttoned to his neck.

"You guys drove here all the way from Florida? Did you already have a coat for him?"

Greg took a drink of his coffee. "I had some jackets for him, but I had to stop in North Carolina to buy him a winter coat." He shrugged the heavy jacket around his shoulders. "I had to buy one for me, too. It's cold up here." He shivered for effect.

"I think the high yesterday was thirty-eight degrees, so it's cold."

He laughed. "And we didn't even see snow. What use is the cold weather if you can't see snow?"

The doctor breezed into her room, and with barely a glance at the occupants, listed her injuries, the care for them, and told her she would be discharged soon. When he was gone, Paige asked Greg, "Where did my father and his girlfriend go? I think he wanted me to go home with him."

"I could take you home," Greg said.

Paige tried to shake her head and realized she'd have to tell him with her words. "No. It's too dangerous for you and Alan. Whoever hit me with the rock could come back and do something worse."

Her father stalked into the room. She wasn't sure what he thought about Greg, but the two men nodded at one another. She guessed they had met when she was sleeping, and she wondered how Greg had explained their involvement.

"Thank you for watching over my daughter this morning," he said.

"It was my pleasure, sir."

Paige was impressed with Greg's manners, and she hoped they went a long way with her father. Trish winked at her, but she couldn't tell if it was over their current exchange or a previous one. She could have been congratulating Paige on finding a handsome man to run to her rescue.

"I can take it from here," he added gruffly.

Trish touched his arm. "Jim, Greg drove up from Florida to make sure Paige was okay. You can't run him off like Lewis Novak."

Paige cringed when she saw Greg's reaction to Lewis's name. She'd have to explain later that Lewis was in her past.

"I thought I'd have Greg take me to your house," she said. It wouldn't hurt to stop by her house. She doubted anyone would be lurking around until nightfall.

Her father's face flushed, but he nodded. "Fine. I'm sure Trish can whip up something for him and the youngun, too."

Paige glanced at the light outside. "Is it getting close to dinnertime?" She had no idea how long she'd slept.

"I eat at five," her father said over his shoulder as he walked to the door. "I'm old, and I don't like to stay up late."

Greg helped Paige out of bed, and she changed into her clothes in the bathroom. Alan was awake when she came out, but he was still groggy from his nap and late-night adventure.

They drove to Paige's house, and Greg stayed outside his car as she moved through the rooms. She collected her most necessary things, surprised that the house was at a normal temperature. She realized the reason when she inspected the broken window. It had a new sheet of glass.

"My father," she said. He had friends everywhere, and it wouldn't have been hard for him to have paid for it to have been fixed immediately.

She felt better about calling the realtor soon, as there wouldn't be any repairs she'd have to make before the house was listed. She took her bags and went out to the truck.

Greg grabbed the bags from her when she stepped outside. "If Alan wasn't in the truck, I would have gone in with you."

"I know," she told him. "But nothing happened." She shrugged her shoulders, and a pain shot through her head.

Greg's eyebrows drew together. "They really hit you hard, didn't they?"

Paige gave him the directions to her father's house and watched him look around as the road became narrower and the trees closed in around them. He kept looking around like he expected something to jump out at them.

"I'm used to seeing everything around me."

"Don't worry," Paige told him. "The only thing you might meet on this road is some deer and the occasional bear."

Trish had prepared a large meal, similar to the one Paige cooked at Thanksgiving. After Paige showered, she joined them at the table, and everyone ate more than they needed.

Alan's head drooped, long strings of ice cream-coated saliva falling out of his mouth.

Greg put his son in his lap, and the boy rested his head on his father's chest. "I should call a hotel. What's the closest one around here?"

Paige opened her mouth to tell him, but her father spoke first.

"You can stay here. There's no sense draggin' around that child anymore."

Greg looked like he was going to argue until Paige shook her head slowly. He accepted her father's invitation and followed him to a room upstairs where he could put Alan while he slept.

"He's just cautious," Trish said while the men were gone. "He blames himself for what happened with Nathan."

Paige's chin dropped. "Why does he feel responsible? I chose to marry Nathan, and I stayed with him until—"

It dawned on Paige that Trish knew more about her life than she had divulged. Usually, her father had kept the other women in his life separate from her. Even if she saw them, they didn't know much more than her name and age, and as she got older, her profession.

Her father and Greg came back into the room. Her father put his hands on his hips.

"Now, I know young kids like to have fun. I've had a few casual flings in my—"

Paige touched her head. "Dad, I can see where this is going, and I can assure you nothing like that will happen tonight. My head still hurts."

He put his hand up. "Still, it's not good for the youngster to" — he searched for the right way to say how he felt — "hear things that he shouldn't."

A grin stretched across Trish's face. "I guess that means it will be quiet in our room tonight, too."

Without missing a beat, her father replied, "Now, our room is downstairs, so—"

"Yuck!" Paige cried, covering her eyes as if it would shield her from what she'd heard.

Her father left the room and Trish declined help when Paige asked about cleaning up. She nodded in Greg's direction. He was just out of earshot, reviewing her father's train collection.

"You need to spend some time with him while you can," Trish counseled. "I had a long-distance relationship once, and it was better when we really got to know each other."

Paige followed her advice, asking Greg to watch a movie with her. She purposely chose a bad one, and her plan almost backfired when Greg started to fall asleep.

She snuggled up next to him, feeling his heartbeat speed up. She wanted to talk to him and clarify their relationship, but there was a mischievous gleam in his eye. Whether it was because they hadn't explored each other's bodies enough or her father forbade it, the physical attraction reached a new level of intensity.

She thought her head would ache, but she almost forgot about it. Greg's skin on hers relieved her pain more than any medicine.

Paige felt like a teenager as she listened for creaks and pops that would signal another person nearby. When they had found the easiest way to satisfy their needs with the lowest amount of noise, the heat kicked on and startled both of them. Once they knew they hadn't been caught, Greg's desire for her multiplied, and she didn't know how the rest of the house didn't hear them.

Lying on the couch afterward, she let Greg stroke her hair. He was careful not to touch the area around her injury, and she was almost asleep when he moved beneath her.

His action got her attention, and she raised her sleepy eyes. "Are you ready to go to bed?"

He scrubbed his face, and she was reminded that he'd driven almost half a day to see her, sacrificing his sleep. He kissed her deeply before they dis-entwined.

Paige laughed at the situation. "I wonder when we'll actually sleep in a bed together overnight."

"Between my son and your father, it's turning into a challenge," he replied. "And I thought sneaking around would stop when I was an adult."

She pecked his lips. "It made it more exciting."

He walked her to her room and caressed her face before he slipped back down the hall. She wanted to go after him, but she climbed into her bed, wondering how their relationship would work.

Chapter 22

Small feet pounded down the hall, and the door to her room burst open. Before she could register the situation, Alan had jumped on her bed. Greg's irritated voice called down the hall.

"Stop, Alan!"

When he saw Alan was on the bed with her, his features reshuffled from annoyed to horrified. He hurried to remove his son from her bedroom.

"Hey, buddy. I know you're excited, but we can't jump on a lady's bed."

Fully dressed, she tossed her covers down to show Greg he didn't have to worry. "Why's he so excited?"

"Snow!" Alan belted out, wriggling out of his father's grasp, and tearing down the hall. "You have to see it!"

The frozen white stuff had inconvenienced Paige many times, so she wasn't as enthusiastic when she saw more than several inches of it had fallen overnight. She followed Alan's high spirits down the stairs.

Alan ran to the door and slung it open. He dove onto the ground, making snow angels with his face buried in the snow. After less than a minute, he ran back to where Paige and Greg were standing.

"It's c-cold," he said, shivering.

Greg ruffled Alan's hair, and flakes of snow sprinkled out of it. "It doesn't snow when it's warm."

Greg had brought a small backpack with them, and while he retrieved it from the truck, Paige told Alan about all the fun she'd had in the snow when she was his age. In the span of ninety seconds, Alan had grown even more excited about his day.

"Dad, we have to go sledding and build a snowman!" Alan exclaimed.

Greg smiled at Paige. "I wanted to sit by the fire and watch Christmas movies, but I can see I'm outvoted on that one."

Alan flew through breakfast, telling Trish about his first experience with snow and recounting it when Paige's father joined them. Her father listened attentively to him and suggested the best hills for them to try when they went sledding.

With the sled in tow, and bundled from head to foot, they hiked up to the spots her father had mentioned. Paige and Greg took turns sliding down the hills with Alan. The boy squealed with the same amount of delight each time the sled picked up speed.

After almost two hours, they were exhausted. They dragged the sled back and took warm showers, meeting in the kitchen for a warm stew Trish had prepared.

Alan napped upstairs, and Greg and Paige settled by the fire. She put on a Christmas movie, but they were both asleep after ten minutes.

Paige's father didn't approve of naps, so he stomped loudly around the house until Paige stirred. Satisfied that he'd made her less lazy, he went to the kitchen.

Greg woke up Alan, and they ate more of Trish's stew. This time, Trish joined them, delighting in the stories Alan shared about his snowy adventures.

Paige looked at her phone for the first time since her concussion, and she found loads of messages from Laura, Rob, Evan, Lewis, and Daisey. She checked them in order of importance, beginning with Laura's texts. Everyone, besides Daisey, was worried about her, and she did her best to ease their fears. She sent each person a message, thanking them for thinking of her and assuring them she was safe and on the mend.

Evan returned her message the fastest, explaining that he'd found out she was okay through corresponding with Greg, and it was much the same with Rob and Laura, as they had conversed with her father. Lewis sent a quick reply, as he was on duty.

Laura invited her to bring Greg to the shop, and Paige thought it was a great idea. She ran it past Greg as they finished eating.

"The snow looks pretty deep," he said.

"This is nothin', her father piped up gruffly. "It's at a higher elevation here. I doubt they got no more than a dustin' in town."

Greg looked at Paige for confirmation.

"He's right. All the snow in town has probably melted."

"Do you have four-wheel-drive on that truck of yours?" her father asked Greg.

"Yes," Greg replied. "I still go muddin' with my friends sometimes, and it comes in handy when we drive into certain places.

Her father nodded approvingly. "You'll need to be back by ten. I lock up the house at the same time every night."

Greg patted Alan's back. "Are you ready to go meet some of Paige's friends?"

He was deep into a game of tic-tac-toe with Trish. "I want to stay here."

Trish put her arm around his shoulders. "If it's okay with you, Alan can stay here."

Alan seemed excited about spending time with Trish and Paige's father, so Paige and Greg quickly jumped into the truck before anyone changed their minds. They were halfway to town before the truck was fully heated.

They spent an hour with Laura and Rob as customers milled in and out of the shop. Laura stared at Greg disapprovingly, and he picked up on it. Paige cut the visit short when she realized how uncomfortable Laura's looks made him.

"She doesn't like me," Greg said when they were back in the truck.

"That's not true," Paige told him. "She's just worried about me. I don't have a good track record with men."

"I'm glad you brought that up. Are you ready to talk to me about Nathan?"

Hearing her ex-husband's name come out of Greg's mouth jarred her. "Why would I want to talk about him?"

Greg inhaled deeply. "He's the reason you jump at loud noises, and I think he's the cause of the rock going through your window."

Paige tried to think of anything she could do to lead him away from the subject. Her street came into view, and she thought of the perfect excuse.

"Could we stop at my house? I forgot something."

Greg pulled into her driveway and followed her into the house. As soon as they were inside, Paige wrapped her arms around him and kissed him. The kiss deepened, and she backed him onto her couch.

An hour later, as they were wrapped in each other's arms, Greg uncovered her ruse. "I like your way of distracting me, but I want to know what happened with your ex-husband."

Paige had her head on his chest, but she rolled over onto her other side. At first, he stayed on his back, but then he moved behind her, encircling her in his arms.

"I'm sorry if it's hard to talk about it. I just want to understand the situation a little better and help you. When Alan and I come up here, we won't be able to stay in this house, because—"

"I'm selling it," she blurted. "I'm selling it, and I'm moving far away, so he and his buddies can never find me again."

She turned into his chest and cried. He held her tightly and kissed the top of her head gingerly when she stopped sobbing.

"He was abusive," she told him. "I couldn't do anything to make him happy. He'd explode over the way I cooked a steak or the temperature outside, and he'd hit me until I cried or bled, whichever came first."

She didn't dare look at Greg. He had stopped stroking her hair, his body rigid.

"I've known people like him, and I've put a few of them in their places."

Paige lifted and shook her head wildly. "No. You don't understand. He's crazy, and somehow, it makes him stronger. I've never seen him lose a fight."

"Probably because he only fights people smaller than him."

Paige gave up trying to argue with him. After a moment, Greg sat up and embraced her.

"Are we going to try a long-distance thing?"

Paige kissed his chin, and his beard tickled her lips. "I want to."

"Okay."

Paige settled back against his chest. "Can you promise me one thing?"

He looked down at her in the dark.

"Can you promise you won't tell anyone about my ex-husband or my PTSD? I've worked really hard to move past it, and I don't want to be judged for it."

"People who would judge you for something you couldn't control don't deserve to be around you." He looked away. "But, yeah. I can promise that I won't say anything about it."

She rested against his firm chest, and they were almost asleep when Paige thought about the time. "My dad wasn't kidding about the ten o'clock curfew. We'd better get going."

Paige crawled into bed that night with thoughts of their budding relationship blooming around her. Closing her eyes, she believed she had finally found the perfect man for her.

Chapter 23

Paige hadn't thought about the days of the week, and when Greg announced he was leaving the next morning, she was dispirited.

"Mom is back home, but I should check on her, and Alan needs to be at school tomorrow."

"I'm sorry he missed Friday," she said.

Greg ruffled his son's hair. "It was a professional development day, so it worked out."

They made plans for her to visit after Christmas, and she walked them to the truck. Alan ran back to hug each of them one more time before they left, and he waved sadly out the back window as he and his father drove away.

Paige went up to her room and pondered taking a nap before she remembered Daisey's message. At the time, she'd been ready to get back to Greg, and Daisey's message didn't have anything to do with Paige's health, so she'd forgotten to reply. She opened the text and scanned it.

Daisey was always available and had phoned Paige many times around midnight, so she had no qualms about calling her publisher at noon on a Sunday. It rang once, and Daisey picked it up.

"Hey, doll. I was just thinking about you."

"What's up, Daisey?"

"We have another interview scheduled." Daisey had adopted a softer voice, and Paige prepared herself for a blow. "It's with a big network."

Paige sighed deeply. "Of course it is."

Daisey's words picked up speed as she tried to explain her decision. "I love our little area, but we need a bigger reach. Evan has fans from all over the world who'll be excited about this project, and you—"

Paige tuned her out to evaluate what to say next. Daisey fluffed her up when Paige and Greg were only meant to boost Evan's fame.

Daisey was still praising her writing when Paige interrupted her. "This is all about Evan, isn't it?"

She paused. "The project helps you and Greg, too. I've heard that the two of you have been hitting it off lately, and he's a good man."

Suddenly, Paige was embarrassed. Not only did her publisher know about her private relationship, but Paige was part of a project that really had nothing to do with her. "I have no interest in riding Evan's coattails. I do fine on my own."

"Of course, doll. Your characters captured the hearts of all the clean romance readers in this area. "

Paige wasn't fooled by Daisey's attempt to bolster her ego. "Yeah, but Evan has women from all over the country falling at his feet."

Daisey switched gears. "Please do the interview. I'll fly us to Florida. I'll even pay for—"

Paige blinked hard. "Florida? What is so important that you have to pack us up and fly to Evan?"

Daisey went back to schmoozing her. "You're such a sweetheart, and everyone loves your girl-next-door face—"

Paige had finished talking to Daisey long before she hung up. "Daisey, I'm tired of playing second—or even third—fiddle to Evan. I'm not doing the interview, and I'm finished with the book. The editors can put in my parts and add my name to it, but I'm done watching Evan go through a long line of women while I try to get work done. It's disgusting."

She hung up without waiting for a reply. Paige was certain that her reaction had jarred her publisher, but Daisey was used to outbursts. She'd dealt with fiery creatives for a long time.

Paige flung herself onto her bed and screamed into her pillow. A knock at her door jolted her out of her mood.

Trish came inside carrying two cups of hot chocolate. Paige took her cup, and Trish sat at the end of the bed, readjusting her position several times, even though she still didn't seem comfortable.

Paige watched the woman's thin, graceful limbs, and she understood her father's attraction to her. She had a similar appearance to Paige's mother, but Trish was kinder and more devoted to the people around her.

"I heard you were upset," she said.

Her statement left the floor open for Paige to talk to her about her woes. Trish probably thought she was frustrated over her situation with Greg, but she had no idea about Paige's work-related problems.

Paige told her a portion of her troubles. "My publisher wants me to do an interview, but I don't want to do it."

"Why?" She only conveyed the question and not a feeling of support or condemnation.

"I don't do well during interviews. I get too nervous."

Trish took a sip of her cocoa. "There's no reason to feel that way. I saw the interview where you walked off stage, and you were doing really well. It was all in your head."

Paige didn't have the strength to go back and watch her first national interview, but her exit had been highly publicized. It was on every social media feed for a week.

"I'm not doing it," Paige affirmed. "She — Daisey, I mean — wants me to help her promote her star client, Evan Donaldson."

"Wouldn't it help your career to be attached to him professionally?"

Paige picked at the blue comforter that covered her bed. "Yeah, but at what cost?"

"It's only an interview," Trish said. "Would Evan do the same to help you in your career?"

Paige thought about it from Trish's perspective. Yes, Evan was a womanizer, but he was helpful. It was nothing for him to promote another author, as in doing so he'd charm the audience and gain favor with another set of readers.

"Yeah."

Trish put her hand on Paige's arm. "Then you should do it."

Paige stared at Trish's hand until she moved it. She wasn't upset at her touch. She was more surprised by it. Her father's girlfriends had pasted themselves to him, hardly giving her a passing glance.

Trish cleared her throat. "Now that it's settled, you should drink your cocoa before it gets cold. I read you don't like coffee, so I thought my mother's old recipe would be a good substitute."

Paige wished she didn't have to ruin the sweet smile that inched across Trish's face, but she had to do it. "Actually, I'm allergic to chocolate." As she watched Trish's happiness crumble, she added, "But I'm sure it's a great recipe. It smells lovely."

Trish's warm eyes filled with tears, and she ran out of the room before Paige could say more. Paige had learned it was best to let women cool down after you upset them.

Paige's slight had been unintentional, but something about how she'd handled the situation had caused Trish to cry. She knew everything would be okay. Trish had been excited about bonding with her boyfriend's daughter, and Paige had somehow hurt her feelings.

"Maybe I should have risked anaphylactic shock," she said, laughing at the cup in her hand.

<h1 style="text-align:center">Chapter 24</h1>

Greg called her later that night. She had told him to phone her when he got home, but by her calculation, he should have been there for a couple of hours.

"Did you have a safe drive?" she asked.

"It was fine. Alan entertained me with stories about your father's knife collection and the different types of cookies Trish could make."

"She is pretty handy in the kitchen."

"Can you cook?" He must have realized his question could be misinterpreted because he rephrased it. "Do you like to cook?"

"I used to. I don't really like it anymore."

"What changed?" he asked, his smile traveling over the line.

"Nothing," Paige spoke briskly in a tone that didn't match her feelings.

"Oh," Greg said, understanding her avoidance. "It has to do with Nathan, doesn't it?"

Paige's silence filled the room. She almost felt swallowed by it.

"We don't have to talk about it," he told her.

She tried to think of any other subject, but she drew a blank. There was nothing else to say.

"I need to talk to you about something else."

This is it, she thought. *This is where he tells me I'm too closed off or the distance between us is too great.*

"Daisey called me."

Paige was instantly defensive, but she held it in. "Oh."

"She told me that you don't want to do the interview."

"I don't."

"It would really help out all of us." She heard the breeze move across the line as he stepped outside. "Some people who read Evan's work would pick up your books."

"I'm going to do it, Greg. I'm just not happy about it."

There was a moment of silence before he spoke again. "We knew we'd be giving interviews when we signed up—"

"*Local* interviews," Paige interrupted. "I never thought a small press would turn into a big-name company just because of one writer."

"Why do you think Daisey holds onto him?" he returned. "He's her meal ticket."

"That's not the only reason," Paige said. "She's still in love with him, and she wants to punish him for hurting her."

"Daisey's a nice—"

Paige laughed dryly. "You would say that."

"What's that supposed to mean?" he barked. "Are you jealous of Daisey?'

"Why wouldn't I be?" Paige shot back. "She's beautiful and elegant, and you left me alone to sleep with her on the night of her party."

"What? I—"

Paige wasn't ready to hear anything more. She ended the call and slung her phone.

Greg called her back, and she ignored it. She kept her voicemail full so he couldn't leave a message.

She wondered if he'd send her a text message, and she was a little disappointed when she didn't receive one. She turned her light off, signaling to Trish that she wasn't in the mood for another heart-to-heart conversation over her killer cocoa.

Paige typed out an email to Daisey on her phone. She agreed to the interview, but she placed conditions on her agreement.

***

When she stepped out of the limo, Petal called after her. "Can I walk with you?"

Daisey was busy on her phone. She had been taking calls since they got off the plane. Paige looked at her for approval, and Daisey nodded.

Covering the receiver, she said, "Take her with you to the waiting room."

Petal matched Paige's steps, as she was used to keeping up with her mother. When Paige walked in, Evan was already waiting for them.

"There's my girl!" He held his arms open, and Petal ran into them. "How was your flight?"

"It was fun!" Petal exclaimed. "Mommy took a nap, but Paige played *I Spy* with me."

He looked up at Paige as he lifted his daughter. "Paige is a good friend, isn't she?"

The door opened, and Paige turned, expecting to see Daisey, but Greg stepped inside. He nodded at her and shook Evan's hand.

Evan kept himself in check in front of his daughter, so he didn't prod them about their distance. He turned to the window and showed his daughter the places in the city that they could see.

Paige took a seat as far away from Greg as possible. She picked up a magazine and flipped through it, while he took out his phone and scrolled.

They hadn't spoken since she'd hung up on him. After she hadn't answered his call, he hadn't called or texted her, so Paige had left it alone. She'd spent the last week in misery, hoping Greg would reach out to her but remaining true to her stubborn decision not to call him.

An anxious woman with a bright smile and red hair piled on top of her head, breezed into the room. She looked at each of them, surveying them.

"Okay. I'm only going to say this once, so listen up. We're going to do the interview at Evan's house in three days. The studio is booked solid, and we don't have a person available until then. Give your name to Sally at the reception desk, and she'll comp your parking."

The woman exited the room, and everyone was left speechless. They walked back down the corridor, and Paige waited with Petal while Greg and Evan received a parking pass.

Greg flipped the parking pass in his hand. "That was rude. I took the day off work to be here."

Paige wondered how many days he'd taken off work to be with her and if he regretted it. She stared at the back of his head as he walked in front of her, wishing he'd look at her and wink or reach for her hand.

"What happened?" Daisey asked when she saw them, ending her call without telling the other person on the line.

Greg told her about the change of plans, and Evan played with Petal while Paige stood awkwardly on the sidewalk. She was relieved when Petal included her in their game.

Daisey raised her voice to repeat her question to Paige. "Will you stay for a couple of days?"

Paige nodded. "It may give me a chance to calm my nerves." She tried a chuckle that came out dry.

"TV is easy," Petal assured her. "Mommy tells me to smile and say something cute, and everyone always tells me how wonderful I am."

"Of course you are," Evan told her, rubbing noses.

Daisey smiled at them, but when she noticed Paige and Greg were staring at her, she looked away.

"So, Paige, you'll ride with me to the hotel, and Greg, you'll go back to doing whatever it is you do with your days." She stopped as if remembering something. "Unless you want Greg to take you to the hotel."

Paige looked up, realizing that Daisey was talking to her. "I'll ride with you."

A rare look passed between Evan and Daisey.

"Actually, I'm going to spend some time with Petal now, so there won't be room for you." Evan pushed Paige to the side as he passed her. "You're going to have to catch a ride with Greg."

Daisey threw out objections, but Evan stuffed her into the limo before her protests mattered. They pulled away with Paige and Greg still on the curb.

Paige didn't even glance at him. She took out her phone and hit an app.

"Don't worry," she said. "I'm scheduling a driver."

He stood behind her, closing his hand over her screen. "Put your phone away. We need to talk, and we can do it on the ride to your hotel."

She didn't want his clean scent to heighten her senses, but her desire to be with him was overwhelming. "Okay."

She got the address from Daisey, and they drove to the hotel. They hardly spoke until he pulled into the parking space.

Greg turned off the motor and put his hands on the steering wheel as if they were steadying him. "I like you, but I can't handle any drama."

Paige huffed. "You think *I* have drama."

Greg's jaw clenched and unclenched. "If you're talking about Daisey, I didn't sleep with her."

"That's not what it looked like on her post."

He seemed baffled but quickly recovered. "I had her take that down."

"Taking down a post doesn't erase what you did."

"I said nothing happened." His voice was a little louder than he normally spoke, and Paige jumped. She had her hand on the door handle when he touched her arm.

He withdrew his fingers quickly. "I'm not trying to upset you. I was just frustrated."

Paige dropped her hand.

"I didn't sleep with Daisey," he repeated. "I had her take the post down when I realized she was trying to make Evan jealous."

"But you were on her bed."

He closed his eyes as if he was gathering strength. "I stayed with her until she settled down. She was a mess over Evan, and I tried to tell her to reconcile with him, but she was stubborn. When she finally fell asleep, I was too tired to drive, so I passed out in a guest bedroom."

Paige knew it was true. She tried to doubt his story, but she was well-acquainted with his character, and it made perfect sense. Greg was a nice guy. Of course he had rescued the damsel in distress.

"Wait a minute," he said. "Is that why you didn't go with me to Nashville?"

Paige nodded. She was surprised when a tear leaked from her eye.

Greg's arms were around her in a breath, and his eyes asked for permission. She kissed him, and the week apart melted away.

They realized they were in a public parking lot when a car door slammed beside them. The occupant shook his head at them, as if he were wondering why they couldn't wait to get inside the hotel before they had a heavy make-out session.

"Are we okay?" Paige asked.

Greg's eyes narrowed playfully. "You did hang up on me."

"What if I promise to make it up to you?"

His eyebrows went up. "That might work."

They almost ran inside, but a visit to the front desk only lengthened the time they'd have to wait. The attendant told them that Daisey had the room key.

Since she was on the same room reservation, Paige got Daisey's room number from the attendant. Paige and Greg took the elevator up to the top floor, using the ride to reawaken some of their anticipation.

Paige was almost out of breath when she knocked, but she straightened her spine and put on a professional smile. Greg put his arm around her waist, but she batted it away."

"What?" he said. "Do you think she doesn't know we're together? She and Evan left us to make up."

No one came to the door, and Paige knocked again. She pressed her ear to the door.

Whispers and rustling fabric echoed through the metal. Paige looked at Greg, and he shrugged.

"I think we interrupted something," she whispered before Daisey opened the door.

Daisey had requested a two-bedroom suite, and Petal napped in one of the rooms.

Evan sat on the couch with his shirt unbuttoned and a drink in his hand. "It's a lot like being caught by your parents, isn't it, Daze?"

Daisey was unamused. "My parents died ten years ago."

He downed his drink. "That should be a buzz-kill, but this is all too hilarious for me to be upset about it." He pointed at Paige. "Look at her face."

Daisey retrieved her purse and shoved a room key card into Paige's hand. "Okay, doll. I'll see you at Evan's house on Friday."

She practically pushed them out the door. They stood for a moment until Greg's phone vibrated.

He swept a hand through his raven hair. "I just got a text from a friend. He wants me to watch the game with him."

Paige tried not to appear crestfallen. "I can see you tomorrow, or another day."

"You could go with me," he suggested.

Paige thought about it. "No. I'll just stay here."

"Come on," he urged. "I want you to go."

Paige let him convince her it was a good idea, and she followed him to the elevator. After a stop at her room, where they stayed much longer than they'd intended, Paige and Greg left for his friend's house.

Paige had no idea she'd be returning to her room alone.

Chapter 25

"My brother is keeping Alan, so you'll have me all night." He threw her a wink that almost made her shiver.

They stopped at a gas station, and she tried to find a song that fit her mood. She was limited to local radio stations, but they were diverse, so she eventually landed on a song.

When Greg came out, he was on the phone, but when he noticed her looking at him, he ended the call. She couldn't help wondering who had been on the other end of the line.

They drove another half hour with light conversation. He never mentioned his phone call, and Paige wanted to maintain the harmony.

They turned down a street with small ranch-style houses on either side. He pulled into the driveway at the end of the subdivision and led them up to the door. He opened it like he lived there, and when the people inside saw him, they threw up their hands and gave a hoot.

Two men reclined in chairs, and a woman sat on a loveseat. It was obvious which man was her husband, as they had matching titanium wedding bands, and she scooted closer to him to allow Greg and Paige a place to sit on the sofa.

"They're ahead by one," the other man told Greg.

Paige understood which team they favored by looking at the score. She followed the players, trying to get a feel for their drive. Each member seemed to be motivated, and the excitement spilled over into Greg's friend's living room.

During the first commercial break, the two men and the woman looked at her as if they'd just noticed she was there. The men appraised her, nodding their approval at Greg.

"Would you like to help me get some drinks out of the kitchen?" the woman asked.

Paige followed her into the next room. The house seemed small, but clean and organized. Just beyond the kitchen, a large dog stood up in a kennel that was almost too small for him.

"He barks at everything," the woman said, opening the refrigerator. "We put him up when we have company."

"He seems like a friendly dog," Paige remarked as the dog swung his tail against the metal cage.

"He is," the woman returned, sticking out her hand. "I'm Loni. My lug of a husband in there is Mitch, and the weird guy across from him is Sal."

"I'm Paige."

"We know," she said, speaking for the two men in the next room. "You're all Greg has talked about for weeks."

Paige smiled. "He talks about me?"

Loni handed her three Moon Walker beers. "Yeah. We can't get him to shut up." She stood up, facing Paige, with two more beers in her hands. "It's kind of adorable. After Jessica bailed on Alan and him, he's not really dated anyone."

Other than Alan's vague mention of his mother, it was the first time she'd heard about Greg's past. She didn't ask questions, though, as to do so would have been prying. Greg would tell her about Jessica when he was ready.

"It's back on," one of the men called.

Without another word, the woman hurried back to the living room. Paige handed a beer to Sal and Greg, understanding that one was meant for her.

Greg twisted the cap on his beer and did the same for Paige. She didn't like the amber liquid, but she took a sip at appropriate intervals.

Greg relaxed against the sofa, pulling her onto his shoulder. After a touchdown, he jumped up so fast Paige's face bounced against the sofa. He high-fived everyone in the room, and Sal shook her in his excitement.

"Guaranteed playoff position!" he yelled after he released her.

Jarred by their enthusiasm, Paige stayed still. She felt welcome and accepted, as if she had just slid into the part of Greg's girlfriend, but she also didn't know his friends, so she guarded her reactions.

Soon after the abrupt celebration, the game ended. Loni grabbed Paige's hand and led her back into the kitchen.

"Okay. Now we can have girl talk." She pulled refried beans and tortillas down from the cabinet. "I know so much about you. I've read all your books."

"Thank you."

Loni stared out the window while she contemplated her next question. "What I don't understand is why the situation with Robert. He and April were so close to declaring their love for each other."

Paige held up her finger. "But remember, Autumn thinks she might be pregnant."

"No. I think that's just a diversion." She put a pot on the stove. "You've made a love block."

"What?"

Loni sighed. "A love block. It's what happens when four people are involved with each other."

Mitch wandered in, carrying marinated steak in a container. "I think that's an orgy."

She flicked a dish towel at her husband. "Not at the same time, you pervert. I'm talking about when one of them can't make up their mind, and other people get involved with feelings."

"Oh, that's boring." He patted Paige's shoulder. "No offense, but I like it better when she reads Evan Donaldson. We have some pretty wild times." He put his hand to his mouth like he was speaking to Paige confidentially. "She likes to pretend she's Cindy in the books."

Just like every other woman who reads Evan's books, Paige thought.

Loni rolled her eyes. "Don't gross out our guest. She doesn't even know you yet."

He grinned. "I guess she got a crash course." He carried the meat to the back door, his dark hair swinging behind him. "I'm pretty blunt."

Loni put a hand on her hip. "I love that man, but sometimes he's too much."

Paige laughed along with her. "I have a friend back home whose husband is the same way. It makes for some interesting conversations."

"Who's interesting?" Greg asked, putting his arms around Paige from behind.

"Laura's husband," Paige answered. "He always has a colorful comment."

"Laura's not far behind him," Greg added.

"I guess that's why they make such a good couple." Paige looked up at him, and Greg kissed her nose.

"I should help Mitch with the steaks."

After he stepped outside, Loni stared at her pointedly. "See. I haven't seen him that way about a woman in years."

As she had no basis for comparison, Paige changed the subject. "What kind of dog do you have?"

Loni glanced at the kennel. "He's an Anatolian Shepard. He's really great with people, but he has a deep bark." She winked at her. "We put him up so he wouldn't scare you."

Paige's eyebrows went up. "I'm not scared of dogs. You can let him out."

Loni moved past her to grab the condiments. "That's okay, honey. My dad suffered from PTSD after he fought in the war. Firecrackers, trains" — she shrugged — "you name it. Anything could set him off."

Paige felt heat travel from her chest to her face. There was only one way Greg's friends could have known about her condition. He had told them.

She excused herself politely and asked Greg to talk with her privately. Mitch and Loni had a garage that seemed to be used for storage more than a port for their cars, so they stood inside it with a warm breeze blowing inside.

"What's wrong?" Greg asked. "Don't you like Loni?"

Paige took a deep breath. "I like Loni, and Mitch is okay. I'm upset with you."

Greg tilted his head. "What did I do?"

He made it seem playful, like it was a game. She wondered if he'd even thought twice before he betrayed her.

"You told them."

"Told them what?" Still unaffected, he took a sip of his beer.

"You told them about my PTSD."

She watched the gravity of the situation dawn on him. "I thought they needed to know. They have a big dog, and—"

"And you could have told me about the dog, and I would have been prepared for it."

He put his hands on the tops of her arms. "Paige, they're good friends of mine. Loni and Mitch won't judge you or try to pry—"

"You broke your word," Paige interrupted. "And you never gave me the chance to work through it myself."

She turned in a half circle, shaking his hands off her. "I walked into a place where I didn't know anyone, and they had already judged me."

He pointed at her. "Now, wait a minute. My friends haven't judged you. You're judging them by assuming they had an opinion about PTSD."

A tear slid down Paige's cheek. "I just wanted to let people get to know me without the label. I don't want them to think I'm crazy."

He huffed. "Good luck with that after how you've acted."

Paige wanted to be anywhere other than with Greg in his friends' garage. She turned around and walked down the drive. She was almost at the mailbox before he called after her.

"Wait. I can take you back to your hotel."

She held up her phone. "No worries. I already reserved a driver. The car should be here soon."

He reached out to touch her, thought better of it, and put his hand in his pocket. "Where does this leave us?"

Paige's blood was still boiling. "You broke your word."

"I'm sorry," he said. "Please come back inside. I'll tell everyone I'm a jerk. I'll even say it was a lie."

Her anger cooled. "You really don't want me to go."

He took a step toward her. "No. I want to spend as much time with you as I can while you're here."

The car pulled up, and Paige recognized her ride. "I need to go back to the hotel. If you want to see me tomorrow, I'll be there."

She got into the car without kissing him. She hoped it made a statement.

Chapter 26

Evan stumbled out the hotel door. He was drunk, and it looked like he might have been crying.

Paige ran up to intercept him. "Do you need me to call you a ride?"

He blinked twice and stared at her without fully recognizing her. "I'm not signing anything right now."

"I'm not a fan," she told him, trying to lift him by his arm. "I mean, I like your work, but—"

He chuckled. "I like your butt, too."

She folded him into a chair. "What happened, Evan? The last time I saw you, you were happy. Did Daisey kick you out of the room?"

At the mention of her name, Evan's face colored. He tried to stand, but he fell against the chair.

"She won't let me see her!"

"Petal?" Paige asked. "Part of my agreement to come down here hinged on her letting you see Petal."

He flicked the shade of a nearby lamp. "She has decided I have too many *hookers*" — he put air quotes around the word — "and they may infect Petal with their promiscuity."

Paige suppressed a laugh. Sadly, it sounded just like something Daisey would say.

"Can I call you a ride?"

He reached for her face. "You can call me whatever you want."

She ducked away. "I need you to be serious. Do you have family, friends, or a girlfriend?"

He put his head in his hands. She didn't think he would answer, but he uttered, "Dead, gone, gone. Petal is all I have left." He looked up, his eyes rimmed in red. "What kind of woman wants to take away the only person in the world I've ever loved?"

Paige stroked his back. "I don't know. I think she's just hurt."

He jolted upright. "I cheated on *her*, not my baby girl."

He was so angry that he wasn't saying Daisey's name. Paige doubted her words would matter, but she spoke them anyway. "Maybe in her eyes, you did."

"That's complete bull—"

"Ma'am?"

Paige had been wrapped up in Evan's tortured feelings, and she hadn't noticed the hotel staff gathered around them. The concierge and a security guard flanked them.

The stout concierge bent slightly to address Paige again. "He can't stay in the lobby. He's upsetting the guests."

Paige gave a resigned sigh. "I'll take care of him."

To her surprise, the security guard helped her take Evan to her room. He tried to walk inside and promptly fell on his face.

Paige tried to tip the guard, but the woman wouldn't allow it. "The experience alone was worth it," she gushed. "I got to touch *Evan Donaldson*." She moved closer to Paige's ear. "And he even tried to feel me up!"

Paige was thankful the guard had been star-struck enough to help her. She hoped she'd keep the ordeal to herself, but it was Paige's experience that if you asked someone to keep a situation confidential, they would tell more people than if you said nothing.

After she closed the door, she stared at Evan's butt in the air. *What was she supposed to do now?*

There was one double bed in the room. If she put Evan in it, she could sleep in a chair or make herself a pallet on the floor.

"Evan?" She shook him, trying to wake him. He had passed out, drooling on the southwestern-styled carpet.

Paige took him by the arms and dragged him to the bed. Once there, she had to use every ounce of her core strength to push him onto the bed. He fell on her once, their bodies tangled in a mess of limbs. She finally put his head on a pillow and covered him with a blanket.

She reached for the comforter that she'd turned down. A hand touched her breast.

"Come back to bed with me," he slurred. "I like to cuddle afterward."

She rolled her eyes and waited for his arm to go limp. Once his fingers slipped away, she folded the comforter on the floor. After she changed, she slipped into it. The floor pressed against her hip, but it was better than sleeping in a chair.

It seemed like she blinked, and it was morning. Voices invaded her peace, and she jumped up. She couldn't see around the partition, so she moved into the short hallway.

Evan stood at the door, half-dressed, scratching his head, and speaking to whoever had knocked. "What's up, bro?"

Paige met Greg's eyes, and she could see the scene unfolding in his expression. Paige was aware it looked like she'd slept with Evan, but she hoped Greg would let her explain.

His eyes narrowed. He wasn't going to believe her. Before she could stop him, he punched Evan.

Chapter 27

Evan, half-dazed, backed away. He moved his jaw back and forth, but it didn't appear broken. Greg took a step into the room, and Paige ran between them.

She put a hand on Greg's chest. "I didn't sleep with him."

"Do you expect me to believe that?" he barked at her. He pointed at Evan's half-naked body. "What would you think?"

"I'd think you had a lot of explaining to do, but I'd let you do it." She crossed her arms. "I remember hearing you out yesterday."

"It wasn't over another woman in my bed." He threw his hands up. "And Evan Donaldson? He's been with every woman in the country."

Evan folded his hands over his mouth, and when he spoke, his teeth were tinged with blood. "Almost. A few are holding out on me."

Greg glared at him.

"Right. I'll just get my things, and I'll be going."

Paige grabbed his arm as Evan attempted to move past her. "Oh no you don't. You're going to tell him how drunk you were last night and how I took care of you."

Evan smiled. "I doubt that will help the situation, but I appreciate your hospitality."

Paige realized her words had damaged the point she was attempting to make with Greg. Instead of backtracking, she accepted Greg's condemnation. It looked bad, but Evan could have helped her.

"You know what, Evan? You can leave. I wish I wouldn't have had the security guard tote you up to my room last night. I should have left you in a drunken puddle on the sidewalk after I found you. Maybe Daisey was right to keep you away from Petal. What are you going to show her about the way women should be treated when you do things like this?"

Evan had been nodding along as if he'd heard her speech many times. However, when she mentioned Daisey and Petal, his features hardened. She let him walk away to gather his things.

"Tell Daisey I won't be at the interview," she shouted at his back. "I'm tired of helping her out, and I'm not going to promote your career."

Greg stood by the door, picking at the frame. He wouldn't look at her, so she tried to appeal to him one more time.

"Evan was drunk, and I let him sleep in my bed," she said. "I slept on the floor. I'm asking you to trust me."

He looked at the fist he had balled up in his other hand and uncurled it. "I don't think I can."

***

Paige was ready to cry, but Evan still lurked in her room. She slammed the door and stormed further into the room.

Evan's back was to her. He stared at the pallet she'd made on the floor.

"We didn't sleep together, did we?"

Paige wanted to launch into him, but she took a deep breath. "No, Evan, we did not. You tried, but I didn't want to."

He turned, raising an eyebrow. "You didn't want to?"

She threw up her hands. "No, you conceited jerk! I saw you drunk and sad in the hotel lobby, and I let you sleep it off in my bed. You weren't exactly Casanova last night." She thought about the security guard. "Although, you gave the security guard a thrill when she helped me carry you up here."

She thought he'd make a cocky comment, but he sat on the bed and dropped his head. "At least I'm good for something."

Paige didn't want to feel bad for him, but she pitied the broken man on her bed. She put a hand on his shoulder.

"Look, Evan, I think—"

"I'm sorry," he said quickly.

It was the first time she'd ever heard him utter those words, and it rendered her speechless.

"As silly as it sounds, I thought you'd taken advantage of me while I was drunk, so I didn't defend you when Greg showed up."

"Didn't you notice you were alone in the bed when you woke up?"

He put his head in his hand. "I was hungover, and he knocked when I was in the bathroom."

She didn't ask him if he'd considered that he'd woken up in a strange hotel room. She imagined Evan had woken up in weirder places.

"Have women taken advantage of you before?" Paige couldn't believe she'd asked him the question.

He nodded slightly before he stood and pasted on an unhappy smile. "So, we didn't sleep together. That's good. Now, I need to call Greg and tell him."

Paige shook her head. "It's useless. He didn't trust me."

Evan plopped next to her on the bed. "That makes it hard." He swayed his shoulder into her playfully. "You could always sleep with me to get back at him."

Paige appreciated his attempt to throw some humor into the situation. She punched him playfully on the arm.

"Tell me what happened," she said seriously. "Why did you get so drunk last night?"

He smiled, showing most of his teeth. It would have been cute, but they were still tinged in pink.

"Gulping down an entire bottle of whisky will do that to you."

Paige's eyebrows went up. "I'm surprised you didn't vomit."

He rubbed his belly. "I have a strong stomach, and I'm a practiced drinker."

"But what about Daisey?" she pressed.

He stared at her. It wasn't the same look he gave her usually—like he was sizing her up. He considered her his friend.

"I messed up." He turned away, looking through the window at the bustling traffic on the highway. "I asked her to get back together."

"And she threw you out?"

He shrugged. "We'd had a good time. We played with Petal until nap time, and then she grabbed me."

"I thought Greg and I had interrupted you guys."

He nodded. "But we got right back to it when you left. It's like that with us. We're either fighting or—"

"So, why wouldn't she want to get back together?"

He shook his head, avoiding her eyes. "I've slept with too many women. She doesn't want me. No one wants me."

Paige put a hand on his back and rubbed her fingers around consolingly. "You're with at least two women a day. Everyone wants you, Evan."

"That's not true." He looked up at her. "She doesn't want me. You don't want me."

His eyes were full of grief over everything he'd lost and his poor decisions. When she didn't protest, Paige could see the glimmer of hope in his eyes dim.

She didn't want to be the cause of someone else's unhappiness. She put her fingers into his hand.

He looked at their hands. When he stared up at her, his cockiness was gone, and she could see the man she imagined Daisey had fallen in love with.

Evan leaned into her, and she met his lips. His kiss was slow and sweet before it picked up an urgency she wasn't ready to match.

"I can't," she told him.

He backed away immediately, breaking all physical contact. "Okay, but you're sending some mixed signals."

"I mean, I don't want to have sex with you yet."

"Yet?"

She rolled her eyes. "You said no one wanted you because you slept around, but I'm willing to date you."

His eyebrows furrowed. "Date?"

"Yes, Evan. Regular people date individuals they're interested in instead of sleeping with everyone in their proximity."

"It sounds like a lot of work."

She shook her head. "I don't like you enough to beg you to start a relationship with me, so maybe I was wrong to propose it. You think dating is hard, but it would be a lot worse for me to have to tame a playboy."

A grin stretched over his face at her reference. "I am a hot commodity."

She sighed heavily. "Never mind. I don't think—"

"I'll do it." He grabbed her hand, and the sincerity was back. "I want to."

Everything inside her told Paige it was a bad idea. "Okay. We'll try it."

"So, what do we do now?"

He seemed so innocent and vulnerable at that moment. Paige applauded her decision to help him.

"You can start by going home and cleaning up," she said, standing up. "After you have some more sleep, you can pick me up for dinner."

"I don't drive," he admitted.

"Of course you don't." She rubbed her temples. "You know how to schedule a ride, so have one bring you over here to pick me up."

"Okay. We can go grab some drinks."

"No," she said firmly. "This will only work if we're both sober."

He jumped off the bed and spun her around. She laughed despite herself.

"See how good that made you feel?' he argued. "That's what it's like to be buzzed with someone. We don't have to get drunk—"

"I'm not good with limits, so I shouldn't drink."

His blue eyes twinkled. "Sounds like it makes you more fun."

She put a hand on his chest. He stared down at her, and something in her expression changed his mood.

"You're right. Let's get to really know each other." He kissed the tip of her nose. "I can forgo the drinking and sex for at least a day."

She swatted him playfully. "Go take a nap. I'll see you later."

He lifted her chin. While she kissed him, Paige tried not to compare the two men or wonder about Greg, but she couldn't help thinking about the way Greg pulled her to him when they kissed, as if he were trying to fuse their bodies into one.

Some of her passion for Greg must have slipped through, as when she and Evan broke apart, he was breathless. "Are you sure you don't want me to stay?"

"Go reserve a ride," she told him with a smile.

After Evan left, Paige stood in front of her window. She had a view of the interstate and the parking lot.

Just yesterday she'd been in that parking lot with Greg, hardly able to keep her hands off him. Everything had been so perfect.

She let her head droop, her hair falling into her eyes. She wouldn't have a special ending with Greg, but she could facilitate one between Daisey and Evan.

Evan didn't see things from Daisey's perspective. Paige understood that her publisher only wanted Evan to prove himself worthy of Petal and her, but Evan mostly rebelled against the vision of a family man.

Daisey didn't need to see Evan with a parade of women. She was already jealous, but that kind of jealousy only led to anger. She needed to see him in a relationship.

If Daisey saw Evan treating another woman the way she wanted him to treat her, it might be enough to have her reconsider her feelings for him. Daisey still loved him, and Paige hoped it was enough for her plan to work.

She had to work carefully, as any ill-timed experience would make her efforts invalid. She thought about the places Daisey had mentioned on their flight and organized her time with Evan in her mind. With any luck, they'd intercept Daisey several times over the next few days.

Her heart pulled in her chest from longing for Greg, but she had a new purpose. She hoped it was enough for her sadness to stay bottled up and not spill into her actions, as she had an almost perfect idea for getting Daisey and Evan back together.

Chapter 28

"The food here is fantastic," Evan commented as the hostess led them to their table.

Paige scanned the room for Daisey, and she was crestfallen when she didn't see her. She rushed through the meal, smiling and nodding in the appropriate places. Evan was his own fan, so he took the lead in the conversation, talking about everything from his leads in high school dramas to a screenplay he'd been writing.

"But I don't know who they'll pick to play Cindy on the big screen," he said. "She's a looker, but she has raw edges."

Paige's mind had wandered, but she picked up the thread of the conversation. "What celebrities resemble her the most?"

He thought about it, leaning back in his chair and stroking his chin. "You know, I can't think of a single person who satisfies the image I've built of her in my mind."

Paige thought about it. "She's you, isn't she? Cindy is you."

Paige remembered the way he'd insisted that her characters were an embodiment of her, and while that wasn't exactly true for Paige, it was for Evan. She crossed her arms triumphantly.

"Yeah," he replied. "I guess Cindy is a lot like me."

After they ate, Paige suggested going to the art museum, but Evan wanted to take her roller skating. She motioned to her silk dress and his suit.

"We aren't exactly dressed for it, are we?"

He had hired a car to take them around for the evening, and he produced a bag. Knowing her date would make a snide comment, Paige didn't ask why he had the bag. The car took her to the hotel, where she changed and rejoined Evan.

The roller rink was busy, but it was easy for Evan to grab roller skates for them. It was almost like the people parted to make way for him.

He was impressed with her skills on wheels. "I didn't know you'd be able to skate so well."

"I practiced a lot on the floors of my dad's house," she told him, yelling to be heard over the booming speakers. "Do you skate often?"

He answered her question by gliding backward and spinning, ending up beside her. "I've been skating since I was a kid."

He left her, and when he returned, a slower song played. He took her hand and skated with her, matching time, even when her movements were shaky.

Paige knew the song, but it didn't affect her like the one Greg had played for them at Daisey's party. She wondered if he was with his friends, telling them about finding her with Evan.

Paige shook the thought from her head. She was determined to fix Evan's relationship with Daisey. She couldn't afford to let Evan know she was thinking about another man while she was with him.

Evan kissed her, and she let herself give in to the kiss. They were in a public place, so he wouldn't expect more to follow.

After the skating rink closed, he took her to an ice cream parlor where the workers sang tunes to them as they prepared dessert. Paige enjoyed the show while she ate and laughed when a worker grabbed Evan's hand and danced around the room with him.

At the end of their date, Evan walked Paige to her door. She kissed him lightly, and he pulled her close to him.

"Can I take you inside?" he asked.

Paige giggled. "I'm capable of opening my own door. Thank you."

He kissed her again, and if she were any other woman, she would have dragged him into the room with her. His lips trailed to her neck, and she pushed him away gently.

He tilted his head and gave her a cocky grin. "I could tuck you in."

"Goodnight, Evan," she said, smiling back at him. "I'll see you tomorrow."

Paige had been completely unaffected by his advances. She showered and scrolled through social media as she sat on her bed.

Daisey had been at the art museum, and pictures of her next to pieces of artwork littered Paige's feed. Paige shook her head. She should have insisted that Evan take her to the art museum, but too much pressure would have given away her plan or made her seem rude.

She scanned Daisey's comments and learned that she was taking Petal to the zoo the next day. She was unsure about the time they'd go, but she knew Daisey liked to sleep in, so she guessed they'd be there in the afternoon.

Evan messaged her. He wrote that he'd had a great time and was off to bed. He added a picture of himself that made Paige blush. She didn't respond to the picture, but she typed an upbeat message that relayed her excitement for their next date.

***

Evan picked her up in the middle of the afternoon. He seemed brighter and more cheerful.

"I'll be honest," he told her, "I had a nightcap, but I went to bed alone."

His honesty impressed her, and she thanked him for it. "Were you this forthright with Daisey?"

His face twisted into a sour knot. "Why did you have to bring her up?"

Paige apologized, and they rode on the elevator in silence. When they were in the lobby, he took her hand.

"I shouldn't have bitten your head off. I don't like to talk about her, but yes. I was more genuine with her than I was with anyone else. She didn't find out I'd cheated on her from someone else. I told her."

Paige felt like someone had dashed her with cold water. She walked beside him numbly and got into the car. Evan had hired the same driver from their previous date.

"Where are we off to today?" Evan asked happily.

"Could we go to the zoo?"

A look passed over his face that concerned her, and she couldn't decode it. He told the driver to take them to the zoo, and they talked as he navigated the traffic.

"What's wrong?" she asked.

He flicked the door handle. "It's nothing."

She put a hand on his arm. "If there's an *it*, then something is up."

"The last time I was at the zoo, Petal was with me," he confided. "I like being with you, but I want to be with her." He rubbed his eyes.

"You've done some things I've questioned, but it seems you really love her."

His eyes whipped around quickly. "I do, and I told her mother that I'd give up everything to come back home. I said she could have the rights and the money for all my future books if she'd let me see Petal more than once a month." He motioned at the city skyline. "What is all this worth if I can't share it with my daughter?"

His tears fell silently, and he wiped them away, chuckling. "If Petal saw me now, she'd tell me to 'Buck up, buttercup.'"

"She's as whimsical as her father."

He nodded. "It's funny. I thought I'd have a boy, but God gave me a girl, so I'd learn how to treat women properly."

She thought about her father and his escapades with multiple women. "Funny how that happens."

"Do you want kids?" he asked.

They got out of the car, and Evan bought tickets while she thought about her answer. If she said she wanted kids, he might press her for more particulars about her maternal desires. If she responded truthfully, he could be turned off by her answer. He repeated the question when they walked through the gates.

"I haven't really thought about it."

He tapped her butt. "You better start thinking about it. You don't want to wait too long, or you won't know how to have fun with your kid."

He pointed to a camel ride, and before she knew it, Paige was seated on one of them. It chewed constantly, and it seemed to be the only sound she heard as she went in a circle on its back.

They looked at almost every animal, but Paige finally spotted Daisey and Petal in the reptile room. Daisey's assistant trailed after Petal as Daisey talked on her phone, shouting at whoever had displeased her.

Petal saw Evan and ran to him. The moment he saw his daughter, Evan picked her up and twirled her around.

Daisey ended her call and pulled Petal out of his arms. "What are you doing here, Evan? This isn't exactly your type of place."

"He took me here," Petal argued.

"I asked him to bring me," Paige responded.

Daisey looked at her as if she'd just noticed her. "Hey, doll. Why are you hanging out with this scoundrel? He'll bring down your reputation."

She was joking, and Paige hated to ruin her mood, but Daisey had to know about her relationship with Evan if her plan was going to work. Evan beat her to the explanation.

"We're together. Paige and I are dating."

Daisey's eyes moved between them skeptically. "Dating?"

His features hardened. "Yes. You may not want me, but I've found someone who does."

Daisey busied herself with her phone. "I need to take this," she told them, but the phone hadn't rung or vibrated.

"I want to go with you and Age," Petal said.

The eager look on her face discounted a catty pass at her name. Still, Paige cringed.

"I don't think she'll let me," Evan told her, watching Daisey have a fake conversation.

"I'll ask her," Paige volunteered, and before anyone could stop her, she marched over to where Daisey stood.

"Evan and I are going to take Petal around the park," she told her.

Daisey pointed to her phone and raised a finger. Paige was undeterred.

She looked at the time on her phone. "We'll meet you back here in an hour."

She turned to go, but Daisey put her hand on her arm. As she had suspected, the call had been fake, and Daisey held her phone limply at her side.

Paige waited for a tongue-lashing and braced herself for the worst. Daisey's face fell in resignation, and she let go of Paige.

"Don't let her get too close to the rails."

Paige nodded. "We'll take good care of her."

Evan and Paige took Petal to see the goats, and she laughed as one tried to eat her dress. She squealed and proclaimed that they'd eat anything.

Evan left them at a table next to the turtles. Petal watched one while Evan ordered their food from a nearby cart.

"Are you my daddy's girlfriend?"

Paige jerked to attention, and inspiration hit her. "Not really," she confided. "I'm pretending. I'm trying to let your mommy see me with him so she'll miss him more."

Petal's eyes brightened. "So, you're like a double agent?"

Paige didn't think of playing matchmaker as a covert mission for both sides of battle, but she nodded. "Do you know how I can make your mommy like your daddy more?"

Petal looked at her father's back thoughtfully. "I heard them fight a lot. Mommy doesn't like it when he sleeps with other girls." She scrunched up her face. "It's kind of weird. Isn't it? Why would he want to sleep in someone's bed when he could sleep next to Mommy?"

Paige agreed.

"And he has his robe and slippers at home."

Paige smiled at the way her young mind worked. She put her finger to her lips, but Petal added, "Mommy doesn't want Daddy to make movies out of his books. She thinks he'll leave us forever." She looked at her hands and twisted them. "And she doesn't like it when he leaves his stinky socks on the couch."

Paige laughed. "Well, I can definitely understand that one!"

Evan and Paige returned promptly with Petal in tow. Daisey's assistant had left, and Daisey looked intently at the snakes. She seemed to come back to life when Petal jumped into her arms.

"Can I go out to eat with Daddy and Age tomorrow?" she asked.

Paige didn't remember mentioning an outing, but Evan may have invited her while Paige was lost in thought. She watched Daisey consider the request.

"I'll think about it. We have an interview tomorrow, but we won't be leaving until later."

When Evan took Paige back to her hotel, he kissed her deeply, but there was a change in his desire. It seemed to yearn for comfort more than carnal pleasure, and Paige let him kiss and caress her much longer than she'd intended.

It surprised her when Evan left without mentioning sex. When he texted her later, no pictures followed. It was almost like she'd formed him into one of the sweet characters from her novels.

She should have been happy and hopeful about a relationship with Evan. However, Paige was determined to see through her plan, and she missed Greg too much to consider another real boyfriend. As she had for most nights since they had kissed at Daisey's party, Paige drifted off to sleep thinking about him. When she woke, she cried, wishing that every moment she spent with Evan would have been spent with Greg.

Chapter 29

Evan sent a car for her, even though Daisey had scheduled a limo. Paige took the car and arrived early.

He greeted her with a kiss. Paige looked around his grand house and wondered what her life would be like if she were as successful as Evan.

His library boasted ornate shelves, and an Olympic-sized pool graced his basement, but his house felt empty. Paige felt like she was walking through a museum instead of viewing someone's home. Her house was small, but it was cozy, and she preferred the feeling.

As their heels sounded off wood walls and high ceilings, they discussed their upcoming interview. Paige was afraid to admit her nervousness when Evan remained confident.

"I hear the guy their sending over is good at pulling out juicy stories," he commented.

Paige's thumbnail went to her mouth. "Doesn't that worry you?"

He chuckled. "Nope. I'm an open book."

The tour of his home ended in his bedroom. Paige was a little uncomfortable when he wrapped his arms around her from behind, but she leaned into his embrace.

"You know what tonight is?" he asked.

Paige scanned her brain for something she'd missed. When she didn't answer, he spoke for her.

"It's our third date."

Recently, men had grown accustomed to pressuring women into sex by the third date. It was an understanding that was acknowledged and accepted by society. Paige didn't like the deadline, and she had resisted a third date with several men because of the expectation.

"Who said we were going out tonight?"

Evan didn't pick up on her tone. "You'll probably be flying back tomorrow, and I want you to leave with a sweet memory."

Evan was saying all the right things, but Paige wanted to throw up when she envisioned them in the bed in front of her. To keep Evan in check, and relieve her of the situation, she asked to use his bathroom. To her chagrin, he pointed to the one off the main bedroom.

Paige was relieved when she came out, and he was gone, but her heart fell into her stomach when she heard Greg's voice carry up the stairs. She joined the men quickly, determined she would make the situation as comfortable as possible.

After a brisk nod, Greg ignored her and asked Evan an array of questions about the construction of his house. Paige watched the men, wishing she had spent the last few days with Greg instead of Evan.

Evan seemed to have forgotten about the assault, or the men had worked it out without Paige's knowledge. She wished it had been as easy for her to mend hurt feelings with Greg as it had been for him to do with Evan.

Greg had trimmed his beard, and every hair looked perfectly in place. She wondered if he thought she was pretty in her simple green dress or if he had flushed all his feelings for her.

Paige had been falling in love with Greg, and she couldn't believe so much had changed in a matter of days. She wanted to gain his attention, lead him to a quiet area in the house, and explain everything, but she couldn't risk Evan or Daisey finding out.

Daisey whirled into the room with Petal and her assistant. Petal winked at Paige, as she knew her plan.

Daisey looked captivating in her navy blue dress. It accentuated her premature gray hair and blue eyes.

Petal ran to her father, and he picked her up. Greg smiled at them, possibly thinking about the bond he shared with his son.

Before she knew it, Paige was in a garden of roses, daisies, and marigolds. The camera crew set up in front of the door, barring the exit but providing a beautiful backdrop of the garden.

Paige sat in the chair they provided, and her vision blurred. She regained it immediately, but it worried her. Her hands were sweaty, and she wondered if her face was pale or red as a tomato.

The interviewer sat down in a chair in front of them and said his name. Paige didn't hear it, but when the man who worked on the boom asked for a mic check, she thought she heard him call the interviewer Dale.

People moved around her hurriedly. Petal and Daisey eased into the chaos, allowing themselves to be shifted into the optimal positions. When the makeup artist asked permission to touch up Paige's makeup, she complied by nodding once.

Greg looked at her out of the corner of his eye. *Could he see her nervousness? Would it be clear to the viewers?*

"This will be a pre-recorded interview," Dale began. "If there are any hiccups or blunders, our editing staff can remove them." He crossed his legs and lifted his eyebrows. "However, if you stumble and say something that would interest our viewers, then we reserve the right to run it."

"Don't reveal dirty secrets," Evan said with a wink. "Got it."

"Okay." Dale looked at the small crew behind him. "If everyone is ready, we can start."

Paige felt her heart rate quicken. Blood marched in her ears so loudly that she wondered if she'd be able to hear Dale's questions. She concentrated very hard on her breathing, trying to maintain a half-smile and a steady rhythm.

Full of charm, Dale asked his questions professionally. He was conscious of Petal's age, but it was obvious he was determined to get information from the group of writers. He asked the basic questions about their hometowns and newest releases, but after he established a good background for each of them, he dug deeper.

"Greg," he said. "You write mysteries and true crime, but your novels mention drugs. Does that have anything to do with your ex-wife's battle with addiction?"

Paige could see he was struggling, but Greg provided a smooth answer. "I guess some of my personal life filters into my work, but it only makes it more interesting, right?"

The men shared a forced laugh, and the interviewer turned to Daisey. "Thank you for bringing your little girl to the interview."

"It was part of our agreement," Daisey answered.

So far, Dale hadn't gotten the extra information he had wanted, but it was clear he was working on another angle. "Petal, it must be so fun to travel back and forth between Tennessee and Florida to see both your parents."

Petal looked at her mother before she answered. "Traveling is fun."

Daisey had taught her daughter the secret of lying by omission. It seemed Petal had answered Dale's question, but she had simply acknowledged his comment about traveling. Unfortunately, Dale picked up on it.

"How often do you fly to Florida to see your dad?"

Petal resisted looking at her mother, but her hands tightened in her lap. "I fly down whenever Mommy lets me."

Dale latched onto her statement, and Daisey tensed. "So, that must be at least once a month."

Petal dropped her eyes. "It's not as often as I want to."

Dale leaned forward and cupped her hand. His fake concern irritated Paige. She wanted to do anything to stop him from interrogating Petal, and her mind raced through possibilities.

"Can you tell us how you feel about it?"

Evan grabbed the sides of his chair. Paige knew he was ready to pounce on the man.

"I want to stay with my dad more. He asked Mommy to marry him yesterday, but she won't do it."

It startled Paige when she heard the new information. She had expected Daisey to fall into Evan's arms, but she didn't believe Evan would try to reach out to her while he was dating Paige. Evan cast a nervous eye in her direction, and Daisey colored.

Dale's attention turned to Daisey and Evan. "So, why aren't the two of you getting married?"

Daisey fumbled for a response. "With his current antics, it's not healthy for me to invest my life in him."

"That sounds like a business deal," Dale said.

Evan had been uncharacteristically quiet, but he pounced on Dale's observation. "It's always like that with her." He tried to play it off with a chuckle, but no one joined him.

Dale leaned back in the chair. The interview seemed to be going well for him.

"Paige," he said, zeroing in on her. "What do you have to say about this?"

She gave a quick reply. "I have no opinion of it."

Dale rubbed his chin thoughtfully. "I think it concerns you. After all, aren't you dating Evan?"

The room was so quiet that Paige imagined she heard a bug buzzing on a flower behind her. Then she realized that the sound was coming from her mind.

"She's only doing it to get Mommy and Daddy back together," Petal informed him.

The child had rescued her, but Paige needed to take Dale's fox-like attention off her. "I'm actually in love with Greg."

She succeeded in taking the attention off Petal, but she had placed herself in a precarious situation. Paige tried to think her way out of it, but she couldn't do it fast enough.

"Then why are you sleeping with Evan?"

"We're not sleeping together," she told him. Paige had to reveal her plan, but she hoped to do it to let Daisey see she'd had her best interests at heart. "I wanted Daisey to understand that Evan was ready for commitment, so I went out with him a couple of times."

"And that backfired," Dale prompted.

Paige's eyebrows shot up. "No. It showed her what it would look like if another woman kept Evan's attention for more than a couple of days. She was simply being a friend to me when she declined his proposal."

She could have saved her pride by saying that Evan had been in on her plan, but then Daisey might have thought his actions were insincere. Page was okay with the blow to her ego.

Evan stared at her with respect. Greg looked hard at the flower just to the right of the camera.

"What a good friend you are," Dale said to Daisey. "Now that you know Paige was only dating Evan to make him more appealing to you, will you marry him?"

Daisey had a list of knee-jerk responses during interviews. It was the first time Paige had seen her flustered.

"No. Yes. Maybe." Daisey's head went into her hand in defeat.

"Those are all the possible answers," Dale pointed out. "It sounds like you need a minute to think about it."

He pounced on Greg. "Does this change how you feel?"

Greg jumped to attention. "What does it have to do with me?"

Dale leaned back, and a smile tugged at the corners of his lips. "Now that you know Paige isn't sleeping with Evan, will you start dating her again?"

Paige saw the repercussions of her real-life writer's block, and she wished their situation were simpler. Greg was finished with her, and his reaction showed it.

"How sad," Dale said with a mock frown. "It seems like you're doomed to be the romance writer who can never find romance for herself."

Paige prayed for the interview to end, but Dale wasn't done. To her horror, he continued to question her.

"Do you think your need to fix Evan and Daisey's relationship has anything to do with your failed marriage?"

"No," she said sharply.

Dale pretended to be wounded. "We're just having a pleasant conversation, okay?"

He left no room for Paige to get back at him without looking like a monster, so she nodded. "Okay."

Greg's jaw clenched.

"What happened between you and Nathan Hart?"

Paige gathered her strength. Her throat felt dry, and her hands were clammy, but she was determined to finish the interview gracefully.

"I was a victim of domestic assault, and I caution your viewers to recognize the signs and leave potentially hazardous situations before they develop into an experience that gives them too many mental, emotional, and physical scars. It's never okay for someone to hit you or purposely break your spirit. I've been where many of you are. I survived, and I want you to do better than me. I want you to survive, live your life, and be free."

Paige had delivered a speech that left Dale no choice but to support her. Without revealing too much, Paige had negated all the trash Dale had tried to collect on the writers in front of him.

Dale ended the interview, and the crew started cleaning up. They hurried as if they had somewhere else to be right away, but Dale was relaxed. He extended a hand to each of them.

"No hard feelings, I hope?"

Daisey answered for the group. "We knew what we were getting into when we signed up for the interview."

One of the crew dropped a piece of equipment, and it clanged on the stone walkway. They picked it up, unaware that it had triggered Paige.

One moment Paige was sitting in her chair, and the next moment, she bolted for the door, knocking people and the camera to the side as she struggled to leave.

Paige didn't remember running away, and her next cognitive thought came to her in Evan's pantry. She sat next to a ten-pound bag of potatoes, and cans of food lined the walls around her. People spilled through the open door. At first, they were unclear, but as she focused, she recognized Daisey, Evan, and Dale.

Greg lifted her hand and rubbed it with his thumb. "You're safe, Paige. We're here with you."

Greg was so close that she could smell the coffee he'd drunk before the interview. She touched his face, but her hand dropped just after she made contact.

"What happened?" Dale asked. "Do we need to call an ambulance? Is she mentally stable?"

"It's PTSD," Greg said.

"Was she in the military?" asked a voice Paige didn't recognize.

"No," Greg told him. "It resulted from the experience with the man you forced her to talk about."

Paige was hyper-aware of the paint on the shelves and the fibers in her clothes. Dale's expression softened.

Evan turned around. "Look, Dale, is it? I'll give you whatever amount you want to keep this quiet."

Dale held up a hand. "No need. I won't mention anything after the camera turned off. My mother was a victim of domestic abuse, but she wasn't lucky enough to get away." He knelt down and met Paige's eyes. "What you said during the interview touched me. I didn't know there was an element of abuse attached to your divorce, or I wouldn't have raised the subject. Still, what you said was inspired, and I plan to run national hotlines and websites for victims to contact as you speak about your experience. Is that okay?"

Paige nodded.

Dale reached out to pat her shoulder, thought better of it, and stood back up. "It was my pleasure to speak to each of you today." He turned to Daisey. "Let me know when you decide if you're going to marry the Don Juan of authors."

Petal had left with Daisey's assistant, and Paige was glad she was gone. She felt guilty for exposing the child to her outburst, and she hoped Petal wouldn't be afraid of her.

She lost track of Greg when she was ushered to Daisey's limo. His hand warmed her own until she stepped outside, but then it was gone.

She was awake for her flight, but she didn't remember most of it. She wanted to sit away from Daisey and Petal, even though Petal didn't seem fearful, but the conditions of her ticket wouldn't allow it.

She could have asked her mother to book another flight for her, but then she could have been in Florida overnight. That meant Evan could find her and force her to talk.

She settled into the seat next to Daisey. Petal wanted the window seat, but the view bored her, and she was asleep within minutes.

Paige thought about putting earbuds in her ears a moment too late. Her publisher had waited for Petal to fall asleep before she spoke.

"Why do you care?" she asked Paige.

Paige didn't try to play coy. "I think you and Evan were great together, and now that he's sowed his oats, I think—"

"You think I should just fall back into the arms of the man who cheated on me? What signal does that send to Petal?"

"You sleep with him, though. What message does that send to Petal and Evan?"

She looked at her hands, twisting in her lap. "I'm still human. I'm weak, so I do my best to stay away from him."

"But that keeps Petal away from him, too," Paige countered.

"I haven't found a good balance yet," she conceded. "But after I saw him with you, I thought I could let go a little because Evan was with someone I trusted."

"I don't really have feelings for Evan."

Daisey held up a hand. "I know that now, but maybe if he agrees to some therapy, I can let him see Petal more."

Paige felt a sense of loss. She wished she could have brought Daisey and Evan back together, but maybe she'd helped Petal see her dad more.

"You're a good friend, doll." The pet name Daisey had for her was back, signaling that they had mended their relationship. Daisey grabbed her hand and squeezed it. "Too bad you didn't sleep with Evan, though. He really is good in the sack." She gave her a confidential wink.

Chapter 30

Paige drove across the town line just after midnight. Her father's house was locked tighter than a drum, so she elected to spend the night at her house.

She parked the car in the garage and checked the house before showering and preparing to sleep. She glanced at her phone before she climbed onto the couch. Paige had missed five calls from Evan. Greg had only tried to contact her once.

She checked her texts, hoping to see something from Greg, but only Evan and Laura had left her messages. Both of them said they had an urgent need to speak with her.

She thought it might be too late to call Laura, so she dialed Evan's number. He answered on the third ring.

"Yeah." His voice was thick with sleep.

"I didn't mean to wake you."

"Paige!" he said, speaking to her in the same tone he had before they had dated. "How are you?"

"I'm okay," she told him. "It was only a mild episode."

"I'm glad to hear it," he said. "By the way, are we still together?"

An unexpected laugh bubbled up. "No, Evan. I think that was established during the interview."

"I thought that might be the case, but—"

A female voice whispered groggily. Evan covered the phone too late. When he returned, she was ready.

"It sounds like you're back to your old ways."

"Are you jealous?" he asked hopefully. "I'll give you a chance to prove I should be a one-woman man."

"I'm not jealous," Paige told him. "I'm disappointed. I set you up to return to your family, but—"

"She's not going to do it," he returned lazily. "The woman is set in her ways."

Paige rolled her eyes. "Daisey thinks you should seek counseling, and I agree with her."

Evan didn't come back with a witty retort. "Okay."

"Will you?"

"I'll do whatever she wants if it gets my family back."

Paige sighed. "I don't know if you'll ever get back together with Daisey, but she might let you see Petal more."

"Then it's worth it."

They hung up, and Paige turned off the lights. Her couch felt warm and inviting, and she was asleep within minutes.

***

She woke with the gentle movement of her hair. A smile inched across her face as a hand caressed her shoulder.

"Greg," she said dreamily.

A hard slap jolted her into reality. The sting traveled like ripples in a pond from her cheek down her neck.

"Who's Greg?" Nathan demanded.

Paige scrambled to sit up on her chaise lounge, but Nathan pushed her down. Holding her by the shoulder, he straddled her.

"Willie told me you had someone else, but I couldn't believe it." He inched closer to her face.

In the moonlight, Paige could make out his features. She was familiar with the honey-brown eyes and high cheekbones, but the buzz cut and scar over his right eye were new.

He noticed her looking at his scar, and he touched it. "Yeah. That was my initiation. The men in my cell took turns hitting me, but I never broke."

Paige felt anger swell in her chest. "Neither did I."

He delivered a quick jab to her nose, and she cried out. She struggled against him, but she couldn't get away.

"You break every time," he said triumphantly.

She couldn't grab the site of her injury or wipe away the blood that ran into her mouth. She moved an arm, and he swatted it away lazily.

He had used his time in prison to build his muscles. He felt heavier as his crushing weight pressed her into her couch cushions.

"Where is he?" Nathan demanded.

He produced a knife from his pocket and flicked it open. It was a familiar weapon. Paige tried to appear unaffected by its appearance.

"Don't you want to talk now?" he goaded her. "I saw you on television. You sat sandwiched between two men, and I know you were—"

A set of headlights flashed through the room as a car passed. Nathan's attention returned to her.

"Where is Greg?"

"Florida," she answered automatically, "But you can't get to him."

She didn't feel bad about telling him Greg's state of residence, as it was on his books and website. Nathan had never traveled more than two hours away from their hometown and didn't know how to drive.

A cruel smile inched up his mouth. "I'll pay him a visit later. For now, it's about you and me."

***

It wasn't like the movies. No one rushed into her house to save her right away.

For three days, Paige was under the thumb of her abuser. He hurt her in unspeakable ways, but she couldn't get away.

She formulated plans to escape, but he clung to her tightly. She thought he would go to sleep, and at one point, he seemed to nod out, but he jerked to attention quickly when she tried to move away.

Nathan kept her shades drawn, but he looked out of the slits in the blinds almost all day and night. He wouldn't eat, and she had a hard time keeping food down, so they both lost weight quickly.

Her ex-husband allowed her to use the bathroom and shower. When he wouldn't leave her by herself, she regretted her bodily functions. It was difficult to shave when he was showering with her, and he wouldn't leave her alone. Still, she made sure to clean herself and change her clothes every day. She never knew if it might be her last act.

He dragged her around by the tops of her arms, and after a day of getting jerked around at his will, she developed large purple whelps. She sucked in her breath every time he touched her, as his fingers always found the same places.

Paige looked for her phone, but she couldn't find it. She thought Nathan had stuck it in his back pocket, but she couldn't get to it. She imagined Laura and her father had to communicate with her, but they had no reason to look for her, as she hadn't let them know she was home. They may have thought she was in Florida, sorting out the mess the interview had started.

Nathan went through down times when he'd profess his love and talk about them escaping together. After a few moments, though, he'd revert to rage, throwing things at her and screaming.

Her only reprieve was when he thought she was asleep. He'd mutter to himself but didn't try to wake her until the sun came up. She felt fortunate that the winter nights were a little longer, as she could get away with pretending to be too physically exhausted to move around nine o'clock every night, and he wouldn't wake her until sunrise.

She had broken sleep, for even though her attacker seemed to have an immeasurable amount of energy, she still needed to rest. She'd doze and slip out of a dream when he'd whisper at the window or try to hide from the invisible forces he thought surrounded Paige's home.

She discovered the reason for his instability on the second day she was forced to spend time with him. He showed the drugs to her, and glared at her as he did them.

Paige knew better than to speak up. She'd stare back at him, trying to make her face blank.

"I'm doing this because I love you," he told her. "You need a strong man, and you won't find anyone stronger than me."

By the third day, Nathan was running out of drugs. At least, that was Paige's best guess, as his use had dwindled. He would nod out as he spoke, and Paige would think he was asleep, and then he would jerk back into consciousness and finish his sentence.

As the day faded into evening, Nathan nodded out more frequently. At one point, he stayed asleep for almost five minutes before his eyes popped open. Paige played an obedient victim, and he fell asleep.

Nathan lay on the couch, pulling her down with him. He had shoved them together closely on the shorter part of the sectional couch instead of enjoying a bit of extra room on the chaise lounge. He wrapped one arm around her, and the other hand held an open knife. As his breath expanded his chest, the knife moved up, almost sliding toward her face.

She inched up slowly. She moved her head, careful to keep all other parts of her body still. When Nathan continued to snore, she placed a foot on the ground and one on the coffee table to support herself. Steadying herself, she pulled up slowly, marking every inch as a private victory. She stood up and waited. When Nathan's eyes remained closed, she chanced a step.

A hand grabbed her knee, and she almost fell onto the coffee table.

"Where're ya goin'?" Nathan slurred.

"Bathroom," she said back, attempting to sound sleepy.

At first, she thought he was going to go with her. He tried to get up, but it seemed like he couldn't get his body to cooperate.

"Be quick about it," he huffed. "I'll be..."

She knew he'd be waiting on her, but she hoped he wouldn't wake until she had escaped.

Paige flew down the hall, the carpet camouflaging her footfalls. She slipped her hand through the bathroom door, turned on the light, and shut the door. If Nathan glanced down the hall, he would see that room first.

Paige moved away from the room and into the bedroom. Seconds ticked by painfully as she opened the window and popped out the screen. She expected a hand to pull her back inside when she crawled through, but she made it outside.

Once her bare feet landed in her backyard, Paige's mind skipped over her options and went on autopilot. She breezed down the streets, desperate to find someone. Her toes hit rises of concrete in the sidewalk several times, but it only slowed her a little as the bright lights of town came into view.

Paige decided she'd go to Laura's apartment. She sensed it was late—even though she was unsure about the time—and Rob might be there.

A car turned onto the street behind her, and she panicked. *What if Nathan had gotten into her car and chased her?* Almost certain the driver had seen her, Paige dove into a bush.

The approach of the lights slowed and brightened, and she prepared to bolt down an adjoining street. A car door slammed, and footsteps stopped just shy of the bush.

Paige took off. As soon as she left the cover of the bush, she could hear her pursuer's feet pounding behind her.

"Stop! Police!"

Paige stopped so quickly that her body collapsed on the frozen ground. She stayed still, begging him not to shoot her.

"Paige?"

She risked turning around, and Lewis picked her up off the ground. His eyes widened when he saw her face.

"What happened?" He reached out to touch her injuries, and she winced.

"Nathan," she said.

"Get your hands off her!" a voice thundered.

Nathan appeared behind Lewis, and her ex-husband jabbed the knife deep into Lewis's back. Paige watched in horror as Lewis buckled.

She fell back to the ground and scrambled to get away. Lewis rose quickly and jabbed Nathan under the chin with his elbow. Nathan went down fast, and Lewis pinned him while he put on handcuffs.

Lewis fumbled with the radio while he tried to hold Nathan in place. Nathan kicked and screamed, drawing several neighbors out of their homes.

Paige had little control over her actions as she walked over to where Lewis struggled to maintain a hold on his prisoner. He had a protocol to follow, and the arrest would be invalid if he didn't follow the rules. The knife bounced as it hung in his back, undoubtedly causing him immense pain.

Paige stared at the snarling man who had held her as his prisoner for days. She had no other thought than to end Lewis's struggle with her ex-husband when she lifted her foot and brought it down on Nathan's face.

Chapter 31

Nathan almost got away with everything.

The injury he received when Paige bounced his face off the bottom of her foot led to allegations that the arresting officer had used unnecessary force to restrain him. Sheriff Murphy asked Paige's father to talk to her about confessing to the assault.

"If you don't take responsibility for what you did, Lewis will face charges, and Nathan will likely go scot-free."

After the incident, Paige moved back in with her father and Trish. She felt like she was encroaching on their private moments, but she felt protected in her father's home as she sold her house and looked for another one.

"Won't I get charged with assault?"

Her father smoothed the imaginary wrinkles on his slacks and glanced around her room to think through his answer. "Probably."

Paige picked at the pillowcase on her bed. "Why didn't Lewis just tell them I did it?"

Her father had almost slipped off the bed, so he readjusted his position. "Lewis is still recovering. The knife missed his heart, but it shaved his lung. He's not been officially investigated yet, but the sheriff had to call the TBI."

Paige rolled her eyes. "If I'd known I'd have to serve time for it, I would have completely disfigured him."

Her father met her eyes. "I'm not gonna say anything against it." He reached out to touch her nose, and she backed away before she knew she was doing it. Pain settled on his features.

"I'm sorry," she told him. "It's leftover nerves from the incident."

"It's a reaction to the trauma," he responded gruffly. "I'd wring that boy's neck myself, but he hasn't shown his face to me since I found out he hurt you the first time."

She put her hand on his arm. "I'm okay, Dad."

He huffed. "This never woulda happened if I woulda had a clear head. I got so wrapped up in a woman, and I—"

"Don't you dare." Paige pointed at him firmly. "I like Trish, and you two make a good pair."

He nodded briskly. "She's a good woman, but I'm a father first."

Paige sighed. "You did your job, Dad. I'm an adult, and I can take care of myself."

He looked away. "Maybe."

"You have to concentrate on living your life," she told him. "Why don't you ask Trish to marry you?"

She could only see his profile, but his eyebrows went up. "I think we're straying from the subject here."

Paige got up and took his hand, determined to be positive about her situation. "Fine. I'm ready to admit to stomping on my narcissistic ex-husband's face. You and my future stepmother can take me to the police station."

***

The process took most of the afternoon.

First, her father made sure his attorney was present before Paige walked into the sheriff's station. Next, the sheriff recorded her confession on video and paper.

Sheriff Murphy scrubbed his tired face. "Thank you for doing this, Paige. Since you came down here before they released Lewis from the hospital, we have a chance of convincing the TBI that Lewis followed procedures until his injury got the better of him."

"Are you going to charge me?" Paige asked.

"That's up to Nathan."

Sure enough, when her ex-husband's plans to have his charges dismissed didn't succeed, Nathan charged her with assault. Paige was booked, but because of her father's deep connections, Paige never saw the inside of a jail cell. Her bail was posted, and she was released. Even though she protested, her father paid her bail, and he and Trish took her home with them.

The morning after her arrest, the news blew up, and social media embraced it. Paige tried to ignore it, but her beta readers and reviewers messaged her, and she felt she owed them a response. She told them her ex-husband had kidnapped her, and she had reacted without thinking. Most of the people she messaged were supportive, but a few of them never got back to her.

Paige had a girl-next-door look and way of writing. Her followers appreciated her clean-cut style, so when some didn't reply to her return message, she wasn't surprised. They had traditional views and opinions, and Paige was certain that they wouldn't contact her again. It hurt, but she had bigger problems.

Nathan claimed Paige had abused him after she had called him to stay at her house. Her injuries resulted from defending himself.

Her father's lawyer let her know he had something he could use against Nathan, but he'd have to present it the right way, or it would be inadmissible in court.

Paige had never been in trouble. She'd gotten a ticket for running a stop sign, but as her "rolling stop" wasn't an outright refusal to disobey a traffic law, her father had it erased from her record. She hoped her background and Nathan's arrest record would be enough to argue her case in court. Still, she couldn't help but feel nervous.

Lewis visited her when he got out of the hospital. She was sitting on her bed, looking at the fading sunlight, when he tapped on her open door.

She sat up when she saw him and tried to hold her smile in place. His cheery features were somber, and he walked with a crutch. He had lost at least ten pounds in the hospital, giving his eyes a sunken look. He met her eyes and smiled, but it didn't brighten his ashen face.

Lewis stepped into her room slowly, concentrating hard on each movement, but the perspiration on his forehead betrayed him. It was obvious his trip up her father's stairs had been difficult, and he settled on her bed quickly, lying across it like he used to do when he'd secretly stayed with her.

"You don't have to put on a front for me," Paige told him. "You were stabbed because you tried to help me."

Tears sprang into her eyes, and she hugged him. Lewis moved to embrace her with both arms, and she lay on his chest as she wept.

Paige hadn't wanted to cry, but Lewis's state moved her. Nathan could have killed them both, but Lewis had been injured far worse.

"I should h-have visited you in the h-hospital," Paige sobbed. "I don't know why I didn't."

Lewis wound his finger through a strand of her hair. "It's okay. You didn't need the extra publicity, and reporters were everywhere." He moved, and it reminded her of his injury. "Besides, I was always more into you than you were into me."

She lifted her head off his chest. "That's not true. You broke up with me."

He shook his head. "We never really broke up. You started hanging out with some guy from another school, and that's when I started seeing Caroline."

She rose into a sitting position and helped Lewis up to the head of the bed. At first, he resisted, but he allowed her to take care of him. He dangled his feet off the side of her bed, so he wouldn't soil her comforter, and Paige took off his boots and put them on the floor.

"I wish you would just let me take care of you," she huffed when Lewis wouldn't let her take off his coat.

"Isn't it enough that you got me in your bed?" Lewis said, raising an eyebrow.

The moment was broken when he started a coughing fit. He held up a hand when Paige tried to help him.

"I'm fine," he said, wincing as he moved into a better position. "It's part of the healing process."

"Are you going to be okay?"

He glanced at the window beside her bed. "I'm far from climbing trees and scaling drainpipes to get into your window at night, but I'll be okay."

They smiled at the shared memory. Paige felt a pull to her ex-lover, and she confessed a long-forgotten secret.

"The boy you saw me with was my driving coach."

His eyebrows furrowed. "You dated a driving coach?"

She picked at the seam of her blanket, causing it to fray. "No, I wasn't dating him. My father made me take driving courses after I got caught running a stop sign."

"So, you didn't cheat on me?"

She shook her head. "But when I saw you with your arm around Caroline, I knew it was over between us." She shrugged. "She had a reputation."

Lewis stroked his chin. "Huh. I thought I gave her a reputation." When he saw his joke had fallen flat, he grabbed Paige's hand. "I never would have started anything with Caroline if I would've known you were faithful."

He pulled Paige to him, and she rested next to him. Lewis pulled her again, and before she knew it, they were kissing. After they'd made out for most of an hour, he tried to make a move.

"We're in my dad's house," Paige whispered.

"Shut the door," Lewis laughed. "It's not like we've never done it here before."

She giggled. "This time he knows you're here, and I don't want my dad to get the wrong idea about us."

Lewis turned serious. "I want to be with you, Paige. I'd like to pick up where we left off."

Paige ran a hand through her hair. It would be easy to let Lewis take care of her. They could hide their relationship until after her court date, and he'd support her through a difficult time.

There was a wheeziness in his breathing that stopped her. Lewis had saved her, and even though it had been part of his job, he would have done the same if he'd been off duty.

Paige wanted to fall back into his arms, but she stopped herself. She still had so many mixed feelings for Greg, and she hadn't had the time to sort them out.

"I don't think it's a good time."

She watched his ego deflate. His eyes flitted to the door.

He ran a finger next to her nose. "I'm glad it's not broken." He pulled himself up and tied his boots. "Broken things really suck."

Paige guessed Lewis meant his heart. They had been a good couple in high school, but Paige doubted they'd be able to manage a healthy adult relationship. Paige would always think Lewis was cheating on her, and he might actually do it.

He left gracefully, kissing the bridge of her nose tenderly before he walked out on his crutch. He hadn't been gone for more than five minutes when her father knocked on her door.

"Did you sleep with him?"

His abrupt question threw Paige off balance. "I-I did not."

"Your bed is rumpled," he observed.

She glanced at the crumpled sheets around her. "I made out with him, but we didn't have sex."

Her father winced at the last word. "He said he wanted to thank you for taking the heat off him, but I didn't think you still had feelings for him."

She stared at the spot on her pillow that still had the indention of Lewis's head. "He was my first love, Dad. There will always be a small place in my heart for him."

"He's a cad," her father scoffed. "I'm glad you ran him off."

"I'm not so sure," Paige said. "I may have just lost my only chance for happiness."

"That boy from Florida. He was your chance for happiness."

After hearing about her make-out session with Lewis, her dad wouldn't sit on her bed, but he plopped into the chair by her dressing table. He crossed his legs.

"What happened with him?"

Paige sighed. "It's a long story, but he thinks I cheated on him with Evan."

Her father sat up straighter, his eyes panicked. "You didn't, did you?"

Paige laughed. "No, I think I'm the only woman in America who hasn't slept with Evan."

"Good," her father replied, settling back into the chair. "He probably has every sexually transmitted—"

Paige held up a hand. "Let's not go there. You're still my dad, and it's a little weird."

He nodded in agreement. "But there's still this Greg boy. I want to see you with him."

Paige stared out the window and back at her father. "It's over with him. He lives in Florida, too, so it wouldn't have worked out. I doubt I'd be good with a long-distance relationship."

Her father looked at his hands. "You know I love you being here," he said. "But you don't have to stay in Erwin. You can travel anywhere you want. Live anywhere you want."

Her father's voice had been barely a whisper when he finished. Paige crossed the room and hugged him.

"I may go somewhere else, but I don't think it will be with Greg. He doesn't care about me anymore."

Her father patted her arm. "Just don't give up on him. He misunderstood something that happened between you and Evan. Maybe he'll figure it out."

Paige wanted to lighten the mood. She'd felt doomed since she'd heard her ex-husband was pressing charges against her. Her situation with the court brought a chuckle up from her chest.

"Well, I won't be going anywhere yet. Not unless you want a bounty hunter coming after me."

Chapter 32

Paige was so nervous the night before her court date that no one could comfort her.

Her dad tried to watch a movie with her, but she couldn't sit still. She hopped up and paced in front of the window as if the police would arrive at any moment to arrest her.

Trish prepared a beautiful meal, but Paige could only manage a couple of bites of her fluffy mashed potatoes before she carried her plate to the sink. Trish asked if she wanted to go into town, but Paige declined. They'd have to go past the spot where Nathan had stabbed Lewis, and she wasn't interested in reliving the night she committed the crime that was giving her so much anxiety.

Daisey called while she was looking for an appropriate outfit for the proceedings. Paige was going to let the call go to voicemail, but she answered it.

"Hey, doll," her publisher spoke. "I need to let you know a few things before tomorrow."

Paige nodded and then realized Daisey couldn't see her. "Okay."

"I've talked with my lawyers, and if you're convicted, we're going to have to drop you."

Paige felt like Daisey had knocked the wind out of her. "But I'm supposed to sign another contract with you in the spring, and what about the book I'm writing with Evan and Greg?"

"If the judge dismisses the charges, we can extend the deadline into the summer, but if you go to jail, we'll have to ax the project."

Paige's knees felt weak, so she sat on the edge of her bed. "I thought we were friends, Daisey. You know my situation."

"I'm behind you all the way," Daisey told her. "I would've stomped that jerk's brains out, but you write clean romances, and readers don't want to buy a clean romance that was written by an author with a confirmed history of violence. It just won't sell copies."

Above all else, Daisey was a businesswoman, and she was right. At Paige's last count, she'd lost almost twenty-five percent of her followers on social media, even though she posted some "meet cutes" she'd saved.

"I guess you have to do what you have to do."

Daisey adopted a jollier disposition. "If all goes well, you can stay with us, doll. No hard feelings, I hope."

"Sure," Paige said. There were a few things she wanted to say to her publisher, but she kept them to herself.

She sat numbly on her bed, thinking about several things at once. Her whole life hinged on what the judge said.

She enjoyed writing, but if she was honest, she had thought she'd had a deeper connection with her publisher. It hurt her that Daisey could dismiss her so easily, and she felt she needed to reevaluate her circumstances.

Daisey pushed her to do things she didn't want to do, and Paige had always thought that was something publishers were supposed to do, but after their phone call, she wasn't so sure. If Daisey wasn't really her friend, it seemed she was only pushing Paige to further her business.

Paige wondered if Lewis was the only one who had been stabbed in the back. She felt like she had knives going down her spine.

The doorbell rang, and her father welcomed Laura and Rob. Paige had talked to her friends but hadn't seen them since the last time she'd left for Florida, so she embraced them fully. They took off their coats and shrugged the snow off them.

Paige led them to the dining room, and after a few minutes, Trish carried in a tray of cheese and crackers. Paige's father followed his girlfriend with a bottle of whisky and wine.

The pair left as soon as they dropped off their contributions. Paige's father put his arm around Trish as they left the room.

"Now, I'm lockin' the doors at ten. If you drink too much, you can stay in the guest bedroom."

Rob and Laura did their best to comfort her. They listened to her talk about her fears and were upset when she told them about Daisey's phone call.

Laura munched on a cracker angrily. "That woman makes me so mad! I can get past her crappy move with Evan's contract because it doesn't concern me, but you are my friend. She's a" — she tempered her language for Paige's benefit — "not-nice person."

Paige shrugged. "She said she would have stomped his brains out."

Rob downed a shot of whiskey. "Who wouldn't?"

"If I had the chance, I would," Laura fumed. "What a piece of—" She looked at Paige, much like a dirty-mouthed aunt might look at her niece when she's ready to use foul language.

"You're pretty quick-tempered tonight," Paige observed. "Are you sure you don't want some of this wine to take the edge off?" She held up the bottle and moved it from side to side.

"No. I'm okay." She crunched another cracker and stared at a spot on the wall.

Rob nudged her elbow and leaned into her hair. "One glass isn't supposed to hurt anything."

Laura stared at him as if she were having a pointed conversation with her eyes. His mouth moved in response, and he glanced away.

Paige put the bottle of wine back on the table. "Am I missing something?"

Laura glared at Rob, and he threw his hands up. She turned back to Paige, resigned to telling her whatever she'd been hiding.

"We were going to tell you a long time ago, but you didn't return my message before you flew off to Florida, and then this mess with Nathan—"

Paige's anxiety bubbled over. "What is it?"

Laura fidgeted, rolling one finger around another. "I'm pregnant."

Relief and confusion battled in Paige's mind. "But that's great news. Why do you guys seem so somber?"

"There are some complications." She narrowed her eyes at her husband. "And some people weren't supposed to say anything until after your court date."

Rob threw up his hands and downed another shot.

"What kind of complications?" Paige asked. "Will you and the baby be okay?"

She shrugged. "I don't really know. The doctors think I'll be fine, but I have a blood clot in my uterus. The slightest movement could—"

Paige jumped up from the table. "You came up my dad's road. There are so many bumps!" Tears sprang into her eyes, and her hand went to her mouth as her mind raced with other ways to get her friend safely back to town.

Rob got up to comfort her. "It's not quite like that."

Paige hardly felt his comfort. "What is the likelihood that everything will be okay?"

Laura wouldn't look at her. Rob answered for her.

"She has about a sixty percent chance."

Paige moved away from him and sat down. "Okay. So, we're going to deal with the forty percent one day at a time."

Rob patted her shoulder. "The sixty percent is the chance that something" — he gulped audibly — "unthinkable will happen."

Laura ran a hand through her hair, and her eyebrows drew together. "See, that's why I didn't want to tell her before her court date." She sat back swiftly and crossed her arms. "I knew she'd be upset."

Her friend's jerky actions horrified Paige. She looked at Laura like she was a ticking time bomb.

"You've made it seem a lot worse than it is," Laura said.

Paige stopped short. "What could be worse than this?"

To her surprise, Laura's face crumpled. "Never getting pregnant at all."

Rob rushed to his wife, covering her in an embrace that looked like he was trying to shield her from harm. Paige's heart melted over their bond, and she wished for the same emotional protection in her future.

Paige waited for Rob to release her friend before she knelt beside Laura's chair. "I'll do anything you need me to do."

"I know you will," Laura sobbed. "And that's why Rob and I want you to be the baby's godmother."

Over the years, the title had become honorary, but to Paige, it was full of responsibility. "Are you sure?"

Rob put his beefy fingers through his wife's skinny ones. "There's no one else in the world that we'd trust with our baby more than you."

"It will be my honor to be your baby's godmother." She reached out, and when Laura nodded, she put her hand on Laura's belly. It was hard, but there was no other evidence of the life growing inside her.

"I'll be twelve weeks next Tuesday," Laura told her. "We haven't announced anything, so you're the first person we've told."

"Do you know what you're having?"

Laura laughed, and Rob shook his head. "She's not far enough along for that." He smiled down at his wife. "And I don't think we're going to find out until it gets here."

Laura recoiled. "It?"

Rob rolled his eyes. "He or she."

Laura nodded. "Better."

"That's going to be so wonderful!" Paige gushed. "We'll go shopping for the baby, and I can help you put the crib together."

Rob raised his hand. "I'm paying for assembly at the store. I've heard too many horror stories."

Laura looked away. "We're getting ahead of ourselves. Supposedly, the age of viability for a fetus is twelve weeks, but in my case—"

Paige stopped her. "I'm going to stay positive. If you noticed, I listed a range of things I'd be doing with you, but that hinges on what the judge says tomorrow."

"That's true," Rob said. "But maybe you could get a suspended sentence since you have a clean record."

Both women stared at him, one with fear and the other with disdain. He realized his mistake and backtracked.

"I mean, if they convict you at all. Or, I guess they could drop the charge."

"It's okay," Paige said. "I know I'm in trouble. The lawyer said I have a good chance of serving less than a year before they release me on parole."

"But he kidnapped you!" Laura yelled. She covered her mouth and glanced in the direction of the living room, where Trish and Paige's dad were watching television.

"I know," Paige replied, rising to her feet and moving to the chair opposite her friends. "My lawyer plans to argue that I had been under extreme amounts of duress, but he doesn't know if it will be enough."

"It's the video, isn't it?" Rob voiced.

Paige didn't have the presence of mind to nod. Her thoughts centered on the happiness she'd felt over the onlooker who had videotaped the incident from her front porch.

At first, the recording had been a much-needed answer to her prayers, as it had absolved Lewis of misconduct and solidified the charges against Nathan. However, it also showed Paige deep in thought as she walked over to Nathan and crushed his face with her foot. The video was all over social media and the local news. As she approached her kidnapper, the look on Paige's face made her assault seem premeditated.

"It doesn't look good," she said.

Laura and Rob exchanged a glance, and they both reached out to grab her hands. The three of them sat there for a long time.

Sometimes, everything is said when nothing is spoken.

<h1 style="text-align:center">Chapter 33</h1>

Judge Willis was a woman. To most females in Paige's situation, that would be a good sign, but the judge was hard and firm, and she cast stern looks at Paige that made her feel like she was x-raying her thoughts.

Her father, Trish, and Lewis sat in the audience. Laura had wanted to be there, but Rob agreed with Paige that it would be too stressful for her.

The first part of the proceedings involved Nathan's side of the alleged assault. He clanked into the courtroom in shackles and stared at Paige. She wouldn't look at him, even though her peripheral vision confirmed his eyes boring into her. His attention was only diverted when he was called upon to speak.

Paige had never heard the sniveling tone that escaped her husband's lips. The lies he told boiled her blood, but she tried to maintain a neutral expression.

Nathan's lawyer cited several examples from her books and pointed to the possibility that she had been unfaithful during their marriage. He built his case around the idea that Paige was a manipulative liar, and her ability to tell stories was explainable in the way she wrote her books.

Paige's lawyer brought forth the documents that outlined the domestic assault that had sent Nathan to prison. He pulled out her mental health records, and Paige thought she noticed the judge's face soften when he mentioned Paige's PTSD.

Paige hadn't wanted to speak. In fact, she'd begged her lawyer not to make her do it, but when the judge spoke to her directly, she changed her mind.

"Do you have anything else to add, Ms. Turner?"

Paige swallowed hard. "I do, Your Honor."

Judge Willis waved her hand, indicating Paige should proceed. Paige gathered her courage and spoke words she couldn't remember after she said them. All she knew was that she was speaking from her heart.

"I used to love Nathan." She cringed when she said his name. "But after years of his beatings and degradation, I no longer knew the man in this courtroom."

She folded her hands. "I don't know if he changed or I changed, but he beat me and forced me to—"

"Objection, Your Honor," Nathan's attorney called out.

He was a wisp of a man with dark hair and green eyes. Paige wanted to hate him, but she could tell he was only doing his job.

She didn't listen to why she'd been interrupted, but the judge agreed. Paige resumed her speech from a different angle.

"During the time I wasn't allowed to leave my home, I was threatened repeatedly. Many bad things happened to me, but I won't get into them. I doubt it would help my case anyway. "Nathan held me in my home for three days."

There was another objection, and she waited through it. She rephrased her approach again.

"When Officer Novack found me, I was hiding in a bush. I ran from him, and when he recognized me, he saw I was injured."

An objection flew out, but Paige's attorney was ready. This time the judge overruled it.

She touched her nose. "My nose had been busted, and there were scratches and bruises all over my body. I know there's a video that shows me walking to Nathan as he lay on the ground. If I had a thought at all, it was that I didn't want him to get away. Officer Novack had a knife sticking in his back, and he could have lost his hold on Nathan."

An unexpected wave of tears came over her. She tried to fight them, but they cascaded down her face. Worst of all, her voice wavered, making her sound like a traitor to the part of herself that was determined to stay strong.

"I want to say I'm sorry that I did it." She was almost certain she saw a self-satisfied smile spread across Nathan's face. "But I'm not. If I had known I would hurt him, I would have held back—because I know it can cause trouble—but something inside me broke. I was in a fog when I brought my foot down on his face. No one deserves to be hurt like that, and I'm ashamed I did it." She dropped her head. "But I'm not sorry."

The court dismissed for a short recess while the judge made her decision. Lewis, Trish, and her father tried to get her to walk outside, but Paige stayed in her seat. She was afraid that she wouldn't come back if she left.

She stood on trembling legs when the judge reconvened. She sat down, and a cold sweat covered her body.

"Paige Turner, I was ready to give you an entirely different sentence before you spoke."

The judge's blue eyes stared at her. They didn't reveal her verdict.

"But you have medical records that document your PTSD. Also, the prosecution has given me no phone records that confirm a call or message was placed between you and Nathan Hughes. Those are the two pieces of evidence I relied upon the most in my decision, but the fog you spoke about confirmed my feelings that you had been under a lot of stress before the alleged assault took place."

She held up her hand as if warding off an objection from the prosecution. "No matter how you ended up with Mr. Hart, you had clearly been abused, as your medical report shows many of the injuries could not have been self-inflicted."

Nathan glared at the judge as he could see the direction in which she was edging. Judge Willis ignored him, focusing her attention on Paige."

"I'm dismissing the charges—"

Paige had no idea what else she said. A moment before she got up, Paige thought she should show her appreciation, and she thanked her.

Paige was almost certain that Lewis and her father had helped her down the stairs and out of the courtroom, but she was fully aware of her surroundings when Lewis knelt beside her at the car. He put his hand on her leg, but it wasn't as familiar as he had been when she'd seen him previously.

"I knew it would all work out," he told her.

She fixed the part of her dress that had ridden up when she'd sat down. "I didn't."

"Besides, Nathan is going to jail for a long time. Judges don't take stabbing an officer lightly."

He laughed, but the action made him wince. Paige bent toward him, and he met her halfway. Their embrace was short but sweet.

Paige watched him walk away.

"That will be a good man for someone one day," Trish said as they pulled out of the parking lot.

"Maybe," Paige returned thoughtfully. "But not for me."

Chapter 34

Greg called twice. He'd left a message with Trish when Paige's assault on Nathan blew up on social media, and he'd phoned Paige directly on the night before her court date.

Paige didn't want to talk to him. She was afraid of what he might say, but she was even more concerned about what he wouldn't say. If it was clear he was over her, she'd lose hope, but she really didn't have the possibility of a future in mind. Keeping Greg's calls unanswered was a lot like having a relationship and not having a relationship. If she spoke to him, though, Greg's tone would confirm whatever he had decided about her.

She looked at his social media, but, as always, it was simple posts about his writing. She didn't dare contact him about their writing project, but Evan called and relieved her of that responsibility.

"When do you start training for your next fight?" he asked.

"Probably about the same time when you go from two women a day to just one."

"You had your chance to be the one," he laughed. "I didn't see anyone else for three days when you strung me along."

"It must have been so hard," Paige quipped.

"Absolute murder!"

They shared a laugh before Evan turned serious. "Daisey is putting pressure on me about our book."

Paige rubbed the space between her eyes with her thumb and forefinger. "I know. It's my fault."

"Well, she didn't start asking me about it until after your verdict," he admitted. "Now, she's blowing up my email."

"I'm sorry you have to deal with her," Paige said.

"I do," he said. "But you don't."

There was a shift of air as he moved outside. "You don't have to renew your contract."

The idea was almost liberating. She felt a weight lift she hadn't known she'd been carrying.

"I don't. Do I?"

"Nope," he said. "And better yet, there's a movement in my fan group that's getting some traction with a team of lawyers. They're planning to prove that the contract Daisey made me sign isn't as ironclad as she'd thought."

"That's amazing, Evan!"

"I have another publisher lined up, and I could speak to him about taking you on, too."

Paige wanted to tell him she was flattered by his offer, but she was going to stay with Daisey Flowers Publications. Instead, her mouth moved to convey her true feelings.

"That would be wonderful."

"I'll set it up," he told her. "And don't worry about Daisey. I have a few things that are going to keep her busy until your contract is up."

"More than suing her over your contract?"

He chuckled. "I'm going to try to get partial custody of Petal. I've been seeing a sex therapist, and he's really helped me through some of my biggest problems."

"Really?"

"Yeah. Believe it or not, I've been celibate." He paused for a beat and added, "But I'd be willing to break it if you want to come down to Florida."

At the mention of the state, her mind immediately went to Greg. "I'm sorry, but if I went to Florida, it wouldn't be to your doorstep."

"I know, I know. You're still hung up on Greggy boy." He chuckled. "You know, there's still a catch in my jaw from his left hook."

"He hit you with his right hand, Evan." It was just like him to divert the conversation to keep it focused on him, but Paige didn't mind. She needed a good laugh.

"Oh, yeah. Well, then it must have been that dominitrix—"

"Evan!"

"Okay, I forgot," he said. "My therapist doesn't want me to focus too much on the sexual component of my relationship with women anyway."

Paige tried to end the call pleasantly, but there was a pause before Evan hung up. "Hey."

"I'm still here."

"You're a nice girl," Evan said. "I'm glad you're thinking about leaving Daisey, and I hope you give Greg another try."

She released a sigh from deep within her chest. "He doesn't want anything to do with me."

"I told him we didn't sleep together, and it was clear from the interview that you had no intention of really dating me."

"Look, I'm—"

"It's okay," he said. "What you tried to do woke me up. But I saw the way Greg ran after you when you broke down. He still cares about you."

Paige closed her eyes and massaged her temples. "It doesn't really matter. We live so far apart. It would never work out."

"If you love someone, you'll find a way."

Paige had only said it once, but she relived the moment she'd said it publicly almost daily. It occurred to her that Evan and everyone else in the world knew how she felt, too.

"Are you going to find a way with Daisey?" she asked.

"No. I don't love her," he returned.

After some thought, Paige realized Evan only loved one person enough to find his way. His daughter.

Chapter 35

The ring caught the light on Trish's hand as she brought breakfast to the table. Paige grabbed her hand and stared at the glittering diamond.

"Does this mean what I think it means?"

Trish nodded, her smile lighting up the room. "Your father proposed to me last night."

"When's the big day?" she asked as her father entered the room.

He pecked Trish's lips and sat across from Paige. "We'll probably go to the courthouse later today."

Trish turned away quickly and spooned eggs onto a plate. Paige picked a piece of her toast.

When she finished chewing her bite, she tapped her father's hand. "Is that okay with Trish? I know you like things simple, but she might like to have a bigger wedding."

He glanced over at his fiance as if the thought had just occurred. "Do you want a big wedding?"

Trish placed a plate of bacon and eggs in front of him. "Maybe not a *big* wedding, but I'd like to have our family and some of our friends there."

There was a long pause while her father thought it over. "And I suppose they'll be a reception?"

Trish brought her thumb and forefinger close together. "We could have a small one."

He turned to Paige. "You have that friend who bakes stuff. Can you ask her to put together a wedding cake?"

"Today?"

"No, Princess. I imagine my bride will want to have time to pick out a wedding dress and invite her friends."

Trish was brimming with excitement. "I think I can get everyone here by the end of the month."

"Laura's pregnancy has some complications, but I think she's still baking," Paige said.

Paige watched her soon-to-be stepmom fall into her father's lap. As she covered him with kisses, she wished for the same happiness. She pushed the thought down. She'd focus on her career and leave the romance up to the characters in her books.

***

Her phone vibrated, and she checked it, convinced it was the couple she planned to meet later. It surprised her to see a message from Greg.

```
I tried to call you, but you won't return my calls.
I miss you, but I understand if it's too hard to
be with me. The long-distance thing is a lot, and
even though you seem to do well with him, Alan can
be pretty rambunctious. I just need you to know one
thing: I love you. What you do with that is up to
you.
```

Paige's eyes brimmed with tears. It was the perfect way to end their relationship.

She didn't have a problem with Alan. In fact, she thought he was the best kid she'd ever met, but she didn't know how they could work through a long-distance relationship.

She deleted the message and Greg's contact information. It was over. She was glad for the experience, as it had shown her she could love and be loved again, but she knew it was best to end things before anything more destroyed the image Paige wanted of herself in Greg's mind.

He loved her, and she could live on that for a long time.

***

Paige stood outside the barn. It was a common wedding venue in her town, and she wondered if Trish would choose the site for her wedding.

Lee and Lacey sat at separate tables as she filmed. Lee got up and walked on wobbly legs to Lacey's table. They were both good actors, as they performed in the local theater troupe, so the reenactment of their first meeting was almost flawless.

"Hi," Lee said before he tripped and fell onto Lacey, knocking her to the ground.

They stayed in character, and Lacey jumped to her feet, horrified that her dress had torn. "What are you doing?"

Lee quickly apologized, but Lacey walked out of the scene, still clearly upset. Lee waited at her table until she returned.

Lacey had composed herself and sat beside him. "Why did you fall on me?"

Lee explained his attraction to her, and her face softened when he told her he'd tripped as he'd been watching her and not his feet. The scene ended with their laughing and discussing a future date.

Paige was glad she'd resumed her "meet cutes" on social media. Lee and Lacey's story would be perfect for Valentine's Day.

"I can't believe you kept the dress," Paige said.

Lacey looked down at the tear in the silk. "I can't believe I still fit in it a decade later."

"I can," Lee said, kissing the bridge of her nose.

"You guys are so perfect together," Paige said. "What's your secret?"

Lacey and Lee exchanged a glance. "Lots of love," they said together.

"And compromise," Lacey added as Lee nodded.

"I guess that happens in every relationship."

"More so in ours," Lacey confided.

Paige cocked her head. "It seems like you guys always agree."

"We do now, but it was only after years of arguing over restaurants, finances, and what side of the bed to sleep on."

"And the way to put toilet paper in the holder," Lee added.

Lacey punched him playfully. "I still say it dispenses under the roll."

"Over," he argued with a grin.

They hugged, and the trio walked to the parking lot. Paige longed to ask the question tickling her mind.

"It's really sweet that you guys never gave up on each other."

Lacey looked up at her husband. "When you love someone, you make it work."

"But didn't you have to sacrifice part of yourselves to make it work?"

This time, Lee answered. "Like Lacey said, we made compromises. We gained so much more by settling our differences than we would have by giving up on each other."

Their parting words resonated with Paige. She drove to her father's house while thinking about the way Lee and Lacey looked at each other and the challenges they'd overcome.

The turn that led to her father's house came into view, but she breezed past it and drove onto the interstate. It was going to be a long drive, but she was going to give love a chance.

Chapter 36

Evan answered on the first ring.

"I'm in the city," she cried. "I thought I remembered where his friends lived, but I haven't been to his house, and I have no idea where I'm going, and—"

"Calm down." Evan's soothing voice was so uncharacteristic that Paige paused.

"I have Greg's address," he told her. "That is where you're going, right?"

"Yes."

He read the address to her, and she entered it into her GPS. "Thank you so much, Evan."

He chuckled. "Hey, if I can't have you, at least I can help you profess your love to a good guy."

Paige paused. *Was there more behind Evan's words?*

"You really liked me, didn't you?" The words were out of her mouth before she'd thought about them.

An uncomfortable silence stretched for almost a minute. "Let's just say I understand why Greg fell in love with you."

"Evan—"

"It's okay," he covered quickly. "I have a lot going on with the court proceedings, and when I get Petal, I'll need to give her my full attention."

Paige searched for something to say. "Petal is going to love spending more time with you."

"I hope so," he returned. "I'm kind of boring now."

Paige hated to end their conversation on such a strange note, but she spotted Greg's truck. "I think I'm here."

"Good luck," Evan told her and whispered a goodbye before he hung up.

***

Paige stood outside the spilt-level brick home and waited for Greg to answer the door. Alan's bicycle rested on the sidewalk beside her feet, a T-Rex on the bell.

The door opened, and Paige couldn't speak. She could only look at the man who had won her heart, even though she had been wading through a deep crisis.

"You're here," he said. "How did you find my house?"

"Evan."

Her voice worked, and she wanted to follow it with more, but she was unsure of the right direction. She quickly decided to bare her whole heart.

"I'm sorry I didn't respond to your message. I was going to let it go, but I saw this couple who was able to work through their differences, and I—"

Greg took a step toward her, stopping her thoughts. He reached out and caressed her face.

"I love you, Paige Turner."

That was enough for her.

They fell into each other's arms, and it seemed natural when Alan joined their hug. Hope bloomed in her heart, and she never wanted to let it go.

Chapter 37

Her father twirled Trish on the dance floor and moved his fingers, motioning for their guests to join them. Paige took Greg's hand, and they glided across the floor.

Several songs later, Greg surprised her by playing the song he had requested for them at Daisey's birthday party. They imagined the sky full of stars they had seen that night as they shared a kiss.

"I should have left with you that night," Greg said.

"Definitely," Paige returned. "You might have gotten lucky."

"I'm lucky right now," he said, touching her forehead with his own.

It had taken a little longer to plan the wedding than Trish had foreseen, but she was happy with all the fresh flowers surrounding her during her late spring ceremony. Paige's father and Trish had been married outdoors, but they held the reception in the cool indoor barn where most of the townspeople held large events.

Paige noticed Rob out of the corner of her eye. He had dressed in flannel, and with his full beard and large muscles, he looked like a lumberjack.

Laura had baked the cake, but her husband had made her stay home with her feet up. He was adept at cutting and serving the cake, giving everyone the same level of friendliness as they approached him.

Paige led Greg to the table, and they each took a cake plate. The strawberries in the center made the vanilla pop with flavor.

"How is Laura?"

Rob shrugged. "She's good when I can keep her still. Now that the doctor says the baby will be fine, she's working hard to close the shop and find a little house."

The information was only new to Greg. Laura had taken Paige to a new house almost every day for the past month, but she had finally narrowed it down to two choices. She'd decided to close her bake shop, too. Laura wasn't giving up her dream, but she was ready to be a full-time mother for as long as her baby needed her at home.

"I'm just glad everything's okay," Paige said.

"How's the new publishing company treating you?" Rob asked, handing two more people slices of the cake.

Paige beamed. "They're really great. The publisher looked over all my ideas, and he's happy to let me do a project that blends genres."

Even though Paige hadn't been in the market for a new publisher, Evan had talked her up to the man interested in his work. Three weeks after they'd spoken about her leaving Daisey Flowers Publications, Paige had an offer from Garnet Ridge Publishing. They'd added a sign-on bonus that had made Paige's jaw drop. She wouldn't be officially joining the group until her contract was up, but she only had another week before she could announce her decision.

The noise from the crowd bothered Paige, so she and Greg moved to an empty table. Greg pulled a seat out for her, and the darkened corner afforded them some privacy.

"I've been looking at houses, too," she told him.

Greg raised his eyebrows. "Oh."

"Yeah. And I think I've found one."

She brought up the picture of the Victorian she'd saved on her phone and showed it to him. She held her breath as he scrolled down to look at the details under the photograph.

He nodded approvingly but stopped short. "This house is in Florida."

She waited for it to sink in. When it did, Greg embraced her.

"How soon will you move?"

Paige sat back in her chair and looked around at her friends and family as they danced and laughed while she made plans to leave them behind. "I'm going to wait until my godchild is born, but after Laura's settled, I think I'll be ready."

He noticed the address before he put her phone on the table. "I thought that house looked familiar. It's on the other side of my block. Alan and I pass it when we go on bike rides."

She measured his reaction, looking for signs of displeasure. "It's not too close. Is it? It was the only three-bedroom house available in my price range."

His smile never wavered. "The housing market is tough right now. I've had my house for ten years, and I wouldn't even think of looking for another one now."

Greg was silent for a beat before he spoke again. "Why do you need three bedrooms?"

Paige knew he was gently ribbing her, and he should have been perfectly aware she'd made the purchase with Alan and him in mind, but he succeeded in getting a blush out of her. "Oh, you never know."

He nudged her with his elbow but turned sober when he stared at her father and Trish. "Are you sure you can move? Your whole life is here."

Paige folded the unused napkin in front of her. "I'll be honest. I don't want to leave Laura and the baby. That's going to be the hardest part." She glanced at her father as Trish rubbed cake across his nose. "But Dad will be fine."

He put his arm around her shoulders. "I'm okay with the way things are. If you need time—"

"I'm going to move slowly," she affirmed. "Like I said, I'll wait to move into the house after I've spent some time with Laura's baby, but the new house will give me a place to stay as I make the transition, and my mom found a way for me to accumulate flight miles so I can visit Laura, Rob, and the baby often."

Greg kept his arm around her, but the mood had shifted. *Should she have waited to tell him after the reception? Did he think the house was too close to him?*

"I can't wait."

She looked up at him, and he was beaming down at her. It was such a change from what she had thought she was feeling from him it was almost startling.

He leaned in for a kiss. When he broke away, it lingered on her lips. "It'll be great," he said. "Then they'll be two writers on the block."

Paige laughed, looking into the eyes of the man who had won her heart. "It will be our own little writer's block."

Did you enjoy the book?

If you liked the story, please consider leaving a review on Amazon, Goodreads, Google, and/or BookBub. Your review can help me a lot, even if you write, "I liked it!"

Thank you so much for reading my book. I hope you enjoyed The Writer's Block!

About the Author

Courtnee Howell-Turner is the author of the award-winning My Brother's Keeper. She also crafted the characters in Solomon's Tears, Hollis's Hobby, and the Amazon best-seller, Finding Emma. Courtnee lives with her children in Northeast Tennessee on her own writer's block (though that is only because she is the only writer on the block). She earned two undergraduate degrees and a Master of Arts in Teaching from East Tennessee State University, and she enjoys reading, writing, and any reasonable music. She helps people travel all over the world, and she's delighted companies pay her to live vicariously through her clients' travel. Otherwise, Courtnee spends her days in comfortable chaos, avoiding sweet tea, chocolate, and unannounced visitors. You'll be lucky to find her on social media, but she'd love your positive comments.□

Acknowledgements

My mama would have loved this book. She would have delighted in Evan Donaldson and sympathized with Paige. She would have reminded me she had wanted my middle name to be Page, like in a book. She loved books.

I wish my mama could have read this book. Even though she has been gone for two years, I know she'd encourage me to put the characters I envision into the world. Thank you, Mama, for always supporting my writing.

Tosha always reads my work and finds all the Easter eggs. She notices when one of the characters from my other books pops up and takes the time to provide insight. Thank you, Tosha, for your continued support.

The rest of my children are supportive and happy about my publications. You can spot them in some of my younger characters.

Even though my friend, Lisa, hasn't read my books, we've talked about them. I think she would also like Evan. In a way, the two of them are similar.

Lisa, thank you for being a wonderful friend. You inspired many of my characters, like Gonzo and Monica.

I thank God for allowing me to write. He has given a gift to me, and I appreciate it.

Sweet 15 Designs created the cover. She even changed my name on the cover after my last name shifted.

I thank God for my gift of words and the ability to edit them. I owe any and all success to Him.

I appreciate everyone who reads my work. Please send me a message if you enjoyed my novel.

Also by Courtnee

Pale Woods Mystery Series
My Brother's Keeper
Book One
Courtnee Turner Hoyle

Seventeen-year-old Jerrod Miller has struggled with the guilt of his actions for an event that took place almost a year ago. His friends have abandoned him, his family ignores him, and he lost his best friend. To make matters worse, he was unable to access records that may have revealed his father's whereabouts. His sister, Ella, guides Jerrod as he tries to learn and accept secrets his family has tried to hide. However, a sinister spirit may be influencing Ella's actions, and it has an agenda of its own.

Finding Emma

It's About Time Series

Book One

What if the only anchor to your identity was a tattoo with a name?

David Winsome answers the door to a beautiful woman who can't remember how she ended up on the hill near his family's home. The woman assumes the name on her tattoo, Emma, and blends into the community while questions about her past plague her.

Why is the town familiar, even though no one seems to know her? And why does she feel an intimate attraction to David, even though she just met him?

As Emma accepts her new life and begins a loving relationship with David, a person who claims to know her enters her life. Does this person hold the key to Emma's past, or is there a mystery much deeper than Emma's identity?

Someone has manipulated the events in his favor, and he has a much larger plan in mind.